On The Wings Of A Prayer

Of A Prayer

An Urban Christian Romance

Wayne Colley

ON THE WINGS OF A PRAYER

DEDICATION

God is of course the very first person I'd like to give thanks to for giving me the inspiration and drive to write this work. The next group of people I'd like to thank for their support is my family, friends, and fans. It took all of you in order for this book to happen and for it to be successful.

May the good Lord bless each and every one of you all.

THE STORYLINE

Carmen is a very beautiful sista. She's smart, resourceful, and has a lot going for herself. That all changes for the worse when she hooks up with the wrong boyfriend. Because of bad decisions on her part, she ends up with a broken spirit and a criminal record. Despite all of that, God's still in the blessing business. She's fighting hard to rise above the ashes of her past. Because of her strong faith, humble spirit, and beautiful determination, God might just be ready to hand her the man and the life of her dreams...all on the wings of a prayer.

CHAPTER 1

Lying in her bedroom on her bed, seventeen-year old Carmen pulled the covers over her head as she heard her mother's live-in boyfriend, Michael, starting to yell. She knew what was about to happen. It was the same thing that happened every time Michael started raising his voice at her mama — raising his hands would be next.

None of that phased Carmen though. Yeah, she felt bad that her mama was about to get a beatdown, but she'd learned a long time ago to stay out of whatever was going on between her mama and her boyfriends — her mother had told her to.

Plus, this hadn't been the first time something like this had ever happened. Carmen's mother, Gina, had had many boyfriends over the years. And yep, every single one of them had wanted to put their hands on her.

Carmen placed her earbuds into her ears and started her music to playing. She loved her mother. She didn't want to hear the pain that the woman who'd given birth to her was about to endure. She decided to try to drown out the battle and get herself some sleep.

Carmen got up early the following morning and got herself ready for school. Since her school was only a half-mile away, most mornings she walked. If it was raining, or the weather was otherwise bad, she'd hop on the school bus.

This particular morning, the weather was perfect for Atlanta in late springtime. There wasn't a cloud in the sky and the temperature was pleasant.

Carmen and her girl, Lisa, normally walked to school together. Lisa's apartment complex was right beside Carmen's. Carmen was glad her girl was walking out the front door as soon as she made it to her place. *I ain't got no time for waiting around for her behind today. I have a Civics test this morning and I don't wanna be late.*

Lisa cheesed as soon as she saw Carmen. "Hey, boo. I bet you thought I was gonna be tripping this morning."

"Girl, what else was I supposed to think? Your ass been late almost every day this week — been making me late, too. What I ought to do is just start walking to school without you."

Lisa laughed. "You know you ain't about to start

leaving me, Carmen. You need to quit playing."

Carmen knew her girl was telling the truth. One of the best parts of her day was walking to school in the mornings with Lisa. Carmen and Lisa had been down ever since elementary school. Lisa felt more like a sister to Carmen instead of just a bestie.

They had only been walking a couple of minutes when a car pulled up behind them and began to slow down. Carmen frowned and looked over her shoulder. When she noticed who it was tailing them, the worried expression on her face turned into a nervous, but excited one.

It was Jason Hopper, a.k.a. J-Dog.

Lisa smiled. "Don't look now, boo...but that fool — you know the one you been crushing on — he's right behind us."

"I know he is, girl. I peeped him out the side of my eye."

Jason put on his flashers and rolled down the passenger side window of his Beemer. He slowed down to a crawl to match Carmen and Lisa's walking speed and flashed them a sexy smile. "Hey Doublemint twins, y'all wanna ride?"

Everybody called Carmen and Lisa the Doublemint Twins. They weren't sisters, but they *did* look a whole lot alike, and they dressed a whole lot alike, too.

"I said do y'all want a ride to school? I'm headed that way."

Lisa cut her eyes at Jay-Dog but smiled. She stopped licking her purple lollipop and said, "What your ass doing heading that way? You like twenty years old or something. I know damn well you ain't got no business at high school. You ain't got no classes."

Jason had dropped out of McKinley High five years ago; he'd been in the 10th grade back then. So it was true that he didn't have any classes to take at McKinley. But he sure had some business to handle there. He had to drop off a couple ounces of weed to his foot soldier — a freshman named RayTron. J-Dog got good money out of the students — and a couple of the teachers — at McKinley.

Carmen grabbed the passenger side door of Jason's ride. "Come on, Lisa. Let's roll."

It only took them a few minutes to make it to the high school. Lisa opened the back door and got out of the car, but Carmen stayed where she was sitting in the passenger-side seat."

"Ain't you coming, Carmen?" Lisa asked. "Your ass said you didn't wanna be late today."

Carmen was sitting beside one of the finest men she'd seen in a long time. She'd been crushing on J-Dog ever since she'd first laid eyes on him. She flashed her girl a little smile. "I'll catch up with you in second block, Boo."

J-Dog grinned. "You rolling with me for a little while

today, Shawty?"

Carmen nodded her head. "Yeah. I'm down."

J-Dog handled his business with RayTron. Then he glanced over at Carmen. "Let's roll."

Four Days Later at School:

Carmen followed behind Lisa in the lunch line and grabbed herself a tray. When they finally made it to their favorite table, Carmen's Civics teacher, Mr. Pittman, approached them.

"I don't wanna interrupt your lunch 'cause I know you guys only get twenty-five minutes. So can I talk to you after school today, Ms. Flood? In my classroom?"

Carmen already knew what her teacher, Mr. Pittman, wanted to talk to her about. She'd missed the last four days of his class. Ever since she'd hooked up with J-Dog four days ago on the way to McKinley, she hadn't been making it to school in time to make it to her first class of the day — which was Mr. Pittman's Civics course. She'd been spending the night at J-Dog's upscale apartment and they hadn't been waking up until around 10 o'clock in the morning. School started at eight. Which consequently meant she hadn't been getting to school until about eleven — some days noon.

9

Carmen gave the man a genuine smile. Mr. Pittman was actually one of her favorite teachers. She figured him to be young — about twenty-five years old. And he was fine as he wanted to be, too. Truth be told, Carmen had had a little crush on him when he'd first started at McKinley High two years ago. "Okay, Mr. Pittman. I'll see you around four. Okay?"

Three hours later, Carmen was taking a seat in a desk in the front row of Mr. Pittman's classroom. "Alright, Teacherman... I'm here."

He didn't waste any time. He went right in. "I wanted to talk to you about your performance in my class...and some other things. Now you've been doing really well — up until this week. You've missed the last four days of classes and I suspect I know the reason why. Rumor 'round school is that you have a new boyfriend."

Carmen nodded her head. "I do." That was the only information she gave him on that particular topic.

He stopped drumming the pencil he had in his hand on his desk. His eyes met Carmen's. "You're a very smart girl, Carmen. And you're going places in life — that is if you don't let somebody who doesn't have a future bring you down." He paused for several seconds to let his words take effect. To let them sink in.

He continued speaking. "The school policy is makeup tests need to be taken within three days. You

10

missed your test on Monday. Today is Thursday. I would've warned you — that is if you'd been coming to class. But you haven't. Right now you have a B+ in my class. However, the test from Monday is 20% of your grade for the semester. Missing that one test has dropped your grade from a B down to a D — that's what it's gonna be after I enter in your score of zero over this upcoming weekend."

Yep, Carmen felt bad about all of that. She may not have been the student with the highest scores in her school, but she liked getting good grades. Her hope was to go to college after graduating.

He noticed the look of disappointment on her face. "Now I'm willing to make an exception for you. We have Saturday school tomorrow morning starting at eight. If you can make it here 8 o'clock sharp, I'll let you make up the test — even though it's against policy."

Her eyes brightened up with a quickness. "I can be here at eight sharp, Mr. Pittman. That's the for real truth. I promise you that."

She flashed him a smile and stood up to leave at that point.

"Before you leave, Ms. Flood, don't forget what I told you about not allowing a rotten apple in the bunch to ruin your entire future. Okay?"

She knew he was talking about J-Dog. She nodded her head. "Okay."

11

Three Months Later:

Carmen walked over to the large walk-in closet in the apartment that she now shared with J-Dog. The day she'd first gotten into his car at school, she'd become his number one chick. He'd even gotten rid of his side chicks for her — or at least he'd told her he had.

She'd moved out of her mom's place a month ago. She really hadn't wanted to do it. But seeing that she'd gotten tired of her mom's live-in boyfriend trying to push up on her for sex on the sly tip, she'd decided to go ahead and leave.

Carmen had been fighting off the advances of her mother's men ever since she'd sprouted hips and breasts at twelve. She was tired of it.

She had a brother who was two years younger than herself. But she never let on to him what was going on. That's because she hadn't wanted him to catch a case behind no mess. Therefore, Carmen had pretty much learned to just stay out of her mother's boyfriends' way. She'd learned to make herself as quiet as possible in the house — almost invisible.

She pushed all of those thoughts of the life she'd been living at home from her brain. Then she began getting dressed for her and Lisa's ladies night out on the town.

Carmen pulled up in front of Lisa's apartment complex in the Lexus that J-Dog had given her. She blew her horn to let her girl know that she was out there. Carmen had grown up in poverty, so it felt good being a high school senior rolling around in her brand-new luxury whip. It felt good sporting the nice clothes and shoes that J-Dog kept her in, too.

Lisa wasn't the type of friend who was jealous of her girl. She was happy that Carmen was being well taken care of. She was even happier about the perks that she herself got from being Carmen's bestie. Now that Carmen had hooked up with J-Dog, the two seventeen-year old girls shopped wherever they wanted to, and went to eat at whatever restaurants their little hearts desired. J-Dog had plenty of money from his hustle in the streets. And he liked to keep his woman looking and living nice.

Lisa flashed her bestie a smile as soon as she got into the car. "Hey, girl...where we rolling to this evening?"

Carmen shrugged her shoulders. "I don't know, but you said that you were hungry. I ain't ate yet either. Wanna go to Luigi's? You in the mood for Italian?"

"That's fine by me. I'm kinda surprised you got the time to come pick me up tonight. I figured you and J-Dog would be going somewhere or something. It *is* Friday."

At the mention of J-Dog's name, Carmen frowned for the first time since her girl had sat in her car that day.

Picking up on her bestie's facial features, Lisa said, "Oh... I sense trouble in paradise."

Yeah, there's trouble alright, Carmen thought to herself. She shook her head. "J-Dog been stressed out lately... That's all. Gucci and his homeboys are crowding in on his territory. Gucci got more foot soldiers than J-Dog do. That mean Gucci winning."

"So I guess that means that J-Dog is stressed out?"

Carmen sighed. She nodded her head.

As they came to an intersection, Carmen looked to her right to check for traffic and Lisa noticed for the first time that her girl had a black eye. She'd put concealer on it trying to cover it up, but it hadn't been completely effective.

"Oh hell naw! That nigga been hitting on you, boo?!"

Carmen didn't feel like talking about what had gone down in the apartment that she shared with J-Dog earlier in the day.

"It was just a misunderstanding, Lisa."

Lisa shook her head. "Misunderstanding my ass!

That nigga hit you, boo."

"He was stressed out... That's all. Like I told you, things been getting kinda bad out there on the streets for him. Gucci and his boys knocked off two of J-Dog's top goons last night. They stole about twenty-five grand worth of cash and product from him."

Lisa frowned. "Sweetie... After all that shit your mama went through with men putting their hands on her, I thought you were never gonna get yourself in a similar situation. At least that's what you used to say."

Carmen had figured that exact same thing. She'd always told herself that the second any man put his hands on her, she was walking. However, after the nice lifestyle she'd gotten accustomed to living with J-Dog, she wasn't ready to go back to poverty. Plus, she'd actually messed up and caught real feelings for J-Dog. She was only seventeen, but she knew she was in love. J-Dog had been treating her like a princess up until today.

Lisa placed a hand of concern on Carmen's shoulder. "I thought you weren't gonna live like that, boo."

"I don't wanna talk about it anymore, Lisa. He apologized for what he did and promised never to do it again. I believe him." She smiled. "Aren't you the one who's always talking about giving people at least one second chance?"

Lisa sucked her teeth. "That don't apply to no nigga putting his hands on you, Carmen. You know that." She shook her head. "And don't even start talking that shit about how you love him. Love don't give you black eyes, boo."

Carmen frowned. "Like I said, let's talk about something else, Lisa."

Lisa didn't like the situation, but she didn't feel like falling out with her bestie. *I'm gonna have to talk to her ass later on. She ain't ready to hear me right now. But I don't see how any of this is gonna play out right*.

Conceding defeat for the moment, Lisa placed a tiny smile on her face. "Alright...new subject. Prom's in two months. You decided what color you gonna be wearing, yet?"

Carmen smiled. "Yeah. If I can get J-Dog to agree to wearing purple accents, I'm going with gold and purple."

In her brain Lisa said to herself: *Hopefully in two months from now, she won't even be dating him...living with him or nothing. Hopefully J-Dog will just be a bad memory for her ass. A freaking has been*.

Carmen had enjoyed her girls night out with Lisa. Instead of going to Luigi's for Italian food like they'd initially intended on doing, they'd picked up another two of their girlfriends and hit up Greenview Center — which was a mini amusement park of sorts. They'd had a good, clean time.

She walked into the apartment that she shared with J-Dog around eleven-thirty that night wearing a smile on her face.

"Hey, Bae," she said to J-Dog as soon as she'd closed the front door behind herself.

J-Dog didn't return her smile with one of his own. Instead, he frowned. "Where your ass been, Carmen?"

Carmen frowned, too. "I was having a girls-night-out over at Greenview Center with Lisa, Chardonnay, and Keisha."

He shook his head. "I don't like your friends. They thots. I don't want you hanging out with any of 'em anymore."

Yep, that pissed Carmen off alright. She rolled her neck and held out her hand, palm facing forward. "Hold up, wait a minute, boo boo. You don't tell me who to be friends with. I don't tell your ass who you can hang out with. That shit should go both ways."

J-Dog's eyes got the cold look to them that he usually only reserved for his enemies. "I done had a bad night, Carmen. I don't need to be coming home to my woman popping off at the mouth at me."

"Ain't nobody popping off at the mouth, J."

"Yes you is. You doing it right now. And this is the last time I'm gonna warn you about it!"

17

Carmen shook her head. Then she sucked her teeth. "Boy, please."

She turned around and began walking away. She was totally unprepared for J-Dog grabbing her by the hair. Less than a minute later, she had a left black eye to match her right one. She'd tried fighting back, but J-Dog was stronger than her. Blood was dripping from her lip as she staggered away from him.

With fire shooting from his eyes and breathing heavily, J-Dog barked, "Now get your ass in the bathroom and clean yourself up. You betta have your ass laying butt naked in the bed in ten minutes. I got some pipe to lay."

Yeah, she was more than afraid now. She understood that it was in her best interest to do exactly what he'd told her to do. She quietly made her way to the bathroom in the master suite. In pain and crying, she hung her head and looked down at her own blood dripping into the sink. When she glanced up in the mirror at her face, all broken and bloody — which looked just like her mama's after a fallout with one of her many boyfriends — something in her snapped.

With a crazed expression in her eyes, she ran out of the bathroom and into the closet. She reached into a drawer in there, then marched back out into the hallway.

Pop! Pop! Pop!

As soon as she fired the shots, she dropped the gun onto the hardwood floors with a loud thud. Then barefoot and still bleeding, she ran out into the night.

CHAPTER 2

Carmen woke up with sweat beading on her forehead. She shook her head and looked around the darkened interior of her cell at Metro State Prison. She'd been having the dream again. The nightmare about what she'd done that had gotten her locked up seven long years ago.

J-Dog hadn't died when she'd shot him — although he'd come close to it. Seeing that she hadn't had the money to hire a defense attorney, she'd had to rely on a free public defender. In Carmen's eyes, her public defender had only done the bare minimum necessary in representing her. Consequently, she'd been sentenced to nine years for attempted murder.

Despite the fact that there were plenty of signs that she'd been abused by J-Dog — and she'd only been seventeen at the time — she'd been tried as an adult and convicted.

She pushed the covers off of herself and got out of the bottom platform of the bunk beds that she shared with her cellmate, Atlantis. She reached into her stash and pulled out the tiny flashlight that she'd had her mama to sneak into the facility for her. Then she grabbed her Bible from under her pillow and threw the covers over her head for privacy — because they weren't supposed to have any lights in the room after dark. Her newfound faith in God had been the only thing that had gotten her through the last seven years in lock-down.

"Hey Carmen," Atlantis whispered from the top bunk.

Carmen frowned. "I didn't wake you, did I?" she whispered back.

"Naw. I been up about an hour. You excited about leaving tomorrow?"

Carmen frowned. "Yeah. I am. But I'm a little scared, too. It's been almost a decade since I been on the outside."

"You reading that Bible of yours, ain't you?"

Carmen smiled. "Yeah. You know how I roll... Can't make no moves without God being a part of it."

Carmen figured that the best thing that had come out of her whole incarceration was finding Christ once she'd gotten two years into her confinement. It had been the many positive changes that being saved brought in her life that had made her eligible for early release. She'd been given a mandatory nine-year sentence. For good behavior, she was being let out on parole the following day — which meant only seven years served. The only condition of her release was that she had to live in a halfway house for six months.

Atlantis laughed. Then using a low voice so that the warden wouldn't hear, she said, "You'll be okay, Carmen. You already know this is my third time coming through here." She nodded her head. "I can tell the ones who ain't coming back. And I can tell the ones who is. Jailbird, you 'bout to be sprung from this cage, and I ain't never gonna see your face around these here parts ever again. But I ain't mad atcha. You deserve to be free."

As Carmen walked out of the facility the next day as a free woman, she had Atlantis' words on her mind. *Lord, I pray that she's right*. Somewhere deep within herself, she knew that she was.

An hour later, Carmen was stepping out of the back of the corrections vehicle that had just dropped her off at the halfway house she'd be living in for the next six months. The place was called Halo House.

The middle aged man who'd been driving the car gave her a smile. "I don't want to have to give you this ride again, you hear?"

Carmen smiled right back. "I hear you loud and clear." Then she slung her lightweight bag over her shoulder, closed the car door, and went to meet her destiny.

She was nervous when she stepped into the large, two-story, colonial-style home that had a big wraparound porch attached to it. She didn't exactly know what to expect. But she was happy that at least it was pretty on the inside of her new digs. She could tell that the place was well taken care of. And she could smell home cooked bread. Her stomach began growling in response to that. It had been so many years since she'd set foot in such an environment.

"Hey, honey. You must be Carmen."

Carmen smiled at the middle-aged black woman who'd just walked into the very spacious foyer. "Yes ma'am. I am." She stuck out her palm for a handshake.

The woman grinned at Carmen and shook the hand she'd offered. "I'm Mrs. Ridley. And I run this here place. Me and my husband."

The woman continued smiling. "The prison always sends over a portfolio for people who gonna be living here. I was really impressed with yours, Carmen. You had really good behavior while you were on lockdown. And you tried to be a positive advocate for the other inmates there with you — but in a good kinda way."

Carmen was pleased by Mrs. Ridley's compliment. She wasn't proud of being locked up. But she'd tried to make good use of her time in confinement — at least the last five years of it she had.

Mrs. Ridley continued speaking. "I'm sure your facilitator over at the prison told you you'd be able to live here free for the first thirty days... Then you're gonna have to start paying rent."

Carmen nodded her head. "Yeah. They told me about all of that. They said it would be $100 a week. Right?"

"Yep. But don't worry about finding yourself a job. It's true that you have a felony on your record, but I have a list of places that'll be willing to hire you...despite your past."

That certainly was good to hear, because Carmen had been worried about that. Yes, she had faith that God would help her to find something. But there still had been a niggling worry in the very back of her mind.

"Well let me show you to your room. It's not very big — seeing that we had a contractor come in and put up a wall to divide all the bedrooms in this house in half. But I think most of our residents appreciate the privacy that comes with having a wall in place. Other than that, you'd have to share a bedroom with someone else."

Carmen had just gotten finished sharing a six foot by seven foot jail cell with various other inmates over the last seven years. She didn't care if her new digs was the size of a matchbox. If it meant that she finally had a room to herself, she was all for it.

"I'm more than sure that the room is gonna be fine, Mrs. Ridley."

An hour later, Carmen was lying flat on her back on

top of the bed in her new bedroom. Mrs. Ridley had given her a tour of the home and Carmen did indeed like the place. It was true that the room was tiny, but she loved that too, because she had space all to herself.

Lying there on that twin bed, she began thinking about her mother. Her mama, Gina, had been to visit her only a few times while she'd been incarcerated. That's because somewhere during Carmen's second year of lockdown, her mother had met and married some guy in the military. She'd begun living in whatever city he'd been stationed in. Right now, she was in Stuttgart, Germany.

Carmen frowned. When she'd first gotten locked up, Carmen had been angry at her mother. Carmen had honestly felt like it had been the domestic violence she'd witnessed constantly as a child that had caused her to snap on J-Dog like she had.

Running into Christ had allowed her to forgive Gina for her transgression. Seeing that her younger brother had grown up and moved away from home, Carmen didn't have anyone who'd tell her the truth about whether or not her mama was still living in a domestic abuse type of situation. She certainly hoped she wasn't.

She sighed and pushed all of those thoughts from her mind. Then she decided to take a her first little nap in a long time as a free woman. She'd only been asleep about twenty minutes when that nap was cut painfully short by a banging sound on the wall outside her door.

Wearing a frown on her face, she got out of bed and went to investigate the source of the disturbance.

Opening her bedroom door, she saw a man with his back to her crouched over a toolbox with a hammer in his hand. The back view of the brotha was real nice. He was wearing a white T-shirt and she could see the impression of the muscles of his back rippling through the fabric — and don't even get started on his powerful looking biceps. She shook her head to get those types of thoughts on his appearance out of her mind. *I just got out of prison. My butt needs to be worried about getting my life together, not how good-looking some man is.*

Now that she knew the source of the noise, she was about to retreat back into her room. He was obviously out there working on hanging some decorations on the wall in the hallway. That's all that was going on, it wasn't some type of catastrophe.

Right before she could get the opportunity to leave, homeboy turned around.

A look of recognition quickly came into Carmen's eyes. "Mr. Pittman."

The man smiled then said, "Carmen... Carmen Flood."

Carmen grinned right back. "In the flesh."

26

"You got early release."

Carmen didn't know how her old Civics teacher knew that she'd been released early, but she nodded her head and replied, "Yeah, I got sprung this morning. It was a blessing."

He answered her question on how he knew she'd gotten early release in his next statement. "I ran into your friend, Lisa, a few months ago. I asked her how you were doing, and she told me that you were petitioning to get out."

Carmen Flood had been one of Mr. Pittman's favorite students. She'd worked hard in both of his classes that she'd been in. He'd been sad to hear about what had ended up happening between her and her no-good boyfriend, J-Dog.

Carmen nodded her head. "Oh. Lisa told me that she ran into you the last time I talked to her. And once again, I wanna thank you for bringing my coursework to the prison when I first got locked up. It's because of you that I was able to graduate high school. I didn't get to walk across the stage, but I got a diploma. Thank you again for all of that."

"You're welcome...you were a good kid, Carmen. I wanted to help you in any way I could." His smile finally turned into a frown. "I followed your case. I don't think the sentence they gave you was fair."

Carmen frowned, too. "Me neither. That's why instead of just sitting around while I was locked up, I took advantage of the free college courses that they offered us in jail. I know it sounds crazy that a prison would allow inmates to take college courses, but that's what they did. I was studying law during my time on lockdown through a correspondence school. It was all online...on the internet you know?"

Mr. Pittman was impressed. "You were in school?"

Carmen nodded her head. "Yeah. I got far enough that all that's left for me to do is somehow pass the bar exam. Then I'll be an attorney." Her frown deepened. "But from what I hear, it's hard for people who go the route I'm trying to take towards being a lawyer to actually become one. There's a character test that you have to pass as part of the Bar Exam. Being a convicted felon makes passing that particular test difficult."

"But not impossible." His eyes met hers. "It sounds as if you've been walking a little closer with Christ since your incarceration, Carmen. Would I be right in assuming that?"

Carmen nodded her head. "Yep. It was God's grace that brought me through the last seven years. There's a lot of mess that can catch up an inmate — prison is a dangerous place. From drugs and feelings of hopelessness, to violence and fights that could end with a person losing their life. Tricks don't be playing up in there. But through all of that, God kept me."

He smiled. "Then you should know that all things

are possible through God. Passing the bar and becoming a lawyer is possible for you, too, Carmen."

"Yeah. That's actually been the only thing that's kept me going in my pursuit of the seemingly impossible." She pointed at the hammer in his hand. "Now on a different subject, what is a civics teacher doing in a halfway house hanging decorations on the wall?"

He laughed. "Mr. and Mrs. Ridley are my uncle and auntie. Sometimes they need help around here. They've always been good to me, so I volunteer to help out."

"I have to admit that I haven't met Mr. Ridley, yet. But Mrs. Ridley is good people. I've only known her a few hours and I can tell that."

"Yes, she is. My uncle's good people, too. You'll see when you meet him."

There was nothing else for them to really talk about, so there was an uncomfortable silence between them for a few seconds. Then Carmen finally said, "Oh, okay. I guess I'll see you around, Mr. Pittman."

"Right. See you around, Carmen—," he cracked a smile and added, "—but what I really should be saying is see you around soon-to-be Attorney Carmen."

She smiled. She liked the sound of that. "Yeah."

Carmen closed her bedroom door behind herself. She knew she had a silly-looking little grin on her face.

"Dang," she whispered under her breath. "Mr. Pittman even finer than he was almost a decade ago when I was in his Civics class."

She also realized at that moment that her crush on him hadn't gone anywhere. She felt like she'd been taken back in time right to the twelfth grade all over again. She sighed and sat down on her bed. "It's just a crush. I'm sure it'll pass."

Outside of Carmen's room, Mr. Pittman was still staring at the door that Carmen had just disappeared behind. *She done blossomed into a beautiful woman—,* he thought to himself, *—despite her circumstances, despite her trials and her tribulations.* He directed his next words towards his heavenly father. *Lord, she's a good person. Please let things work out in her favor.*

The halfway house that Carmen was living in was a ten-bedroom coed facility — meaning both men and women lived there. Later on that afternoon, she met a few of her housemates.

Janelle Bryce, a pretty light-skinned girl with long dreadlocks, gave Carmen a smile as they worked together on cleaning up the kitchen. "I've been here for months. I came straight over from being in lock up at Metro just like you, Carmen. It feels kinda weird living with men again, don't it?"

30

"Yep. In my section over at Metro, seeing a man was a rare thing — we mostly had female security guards or whatnot. On visitation day, there were some men around though... For the ladies who decided they were okay with having male visitors."

Janelle looked at Carmen with an expression of curiosity in her eyes. "You a pretty girl. You didn't have a boyfriend or something visiting you at Metro?"

Carmen frowned. She shook her head. "Naw. I didn't need no man coming to see me."

"I ain't trying to be nosy — all up in your business — but it sound like you got locked up for something similar to why I was locked up. I stabbed my husband. He wouldn't keep his hands off of me. Always roughing me up. One day I snapped."

Carmen nodded her head. "Yeah. I ain't proud of it, but I shot my ex cause he started putting his hands on me."

Janelle sighed. "I did fifteen years. Missed my two babies growing up and everything. After all of that, I really don't feel like dealing with no man — well, not in a relationship type of way." Then she smiled. "But that nephew of Mrs. Ridley. He sure fine enough to make a sista kinda want to change her mind." Her eyes met Carmen's. "You met him yet?"

"Yeah. He used to be my Civics teacher back in high school...not in lockup, but on the outside."

Janelle's grin got a little bigger. "That musta been

31

interesting being in his class. Did you sit up front? You know, so you could get yourself an eyeful?" Then she laughed.

Carmen smiled. "Naw... Well yeah, I was on the second row." She laughed, too, at that point. "All them heifers in my class with me were almost fighting to get all the way to the front. It was crazy. Now I wasn't one to be fighting over being up in no man's face though — I didn't care how fine he was. Same thing applies today."

Janelle skimmed her eyes over Carmen real quick. *I wonder if she down with the girl-on-girl thing*, she thought to herself. *Carmen fine as she wanna be.*

Carmen noticed the way Janelle had just looked at her. She gave the woman a slow smile and shook her head. "Sorry, Janelle. I ain't about that type of lifestyle. Now I ain't knocking you for how you living, but that ain't me."

Janelle grinned. "That's cool, Carmen." Then she winked her eye and laughed. "But if you ever decide to switch teams, give me a call. Okay?"

Lesbianism was against the saved lifestyle that Carmen had decided to live. Therefore she was pretty much sure that she wasn't gonna be giving Janelle that phone call. Since she knew that people weren't perfect, she wasn't gonna judge the girl she'd just met because of her chosen sexual orientation either *Judging is up to the Lord, not me.*

32

Carmen continued about her day. Later on that night, after she'd said her prayers and laid her head down on her pillow, she began thinking about Janelle and her proposition for hooking up for sex and/or a relationship.

Prison had been rough and Carmen had indeed gotten lonely and sexually frustrated while she was on lock up. She wasn't proud of herself, but she'd tried a girl on girl relationship during her first few months of being incarcerated. Being with a woman had never felt natural to Carmen, so it hadn't taken her long to call things off with her prison lover. When she'd decided to follow Jesus about a year after all of that had gone down, she'd repented of her sins. She'd turned a new leaf in her life.

She sighed. Then she reached over and turned on the lamp on the nightstand by her bedside. She couldn't help the smile from materializing on her face. As she picked up her Bible to read, she couldn't help but think: *It sure feels good being able to turn on a light anytime I want to. Thank you Lord for this little blessing.*

She studied her word for the next half hour or so. When she finally turned off the light and closed her eyes, a picture of Mr. Pittman's handsome face flashed up in her mind. *Janelle is right...he sure is fine as he wannabe.*

CHAPTER 3

The next morning, Carmen hit the streets of Atlanta with the list of places that Mrs. Ridley had said would possibly hire her. She was grateful for the 30-day bus pass that the nice middle-aged woman had given her. Not having that would've made it hard for her to make it to the different job locations she was interested in applying at.

Mrs. Ridley had a computer in the study at the halfway house. Carmen had looked up some of the places online; she'd even put in a few applications. But she figured showing up in person would give her a better chance of actually finding a job. Consequently, she spent all of her morning on her job hunting endeavors.

As soon as she got back to the halfway house, she asked Mrs. Ridley if it would be okay if she made a local call on the house phone. With Mrs. Ridley's approval, she dialed her bestie from high school's cell phone number. Her girl Lisa answered on the third ring.

"Guess who got sprung yesterday?"

"Carmen, is that you?" Lisa said excitedly into her cell phone.

"Yep. I made it to that halfway house on Vine Street that I told you I'd be living at. It's called Halo House."

"Girl, give me the address. I'm rolling over. We about to hit up the town to celebrate."

Carmen laughed. "It's a little too early in the day for all that. Plus, I just got through taking the bus all over Atlanta looking for a job. But I do want to see you. I been missing my bestie all these years, boo."

"What about this evening? Let me take your ass to dinner."

Going out to dinner actually sounded like a good idea to Carmen. Mrs. Ridley had hooked her up with a few items of clothing, but it was only casual wear type of stuff. Therefore she told Lisa, "I'm game for that, but nowhere fancy… Okay?"

"You sure, girl? I'm not broke like I used to be when we used to run the streets together. We can go out somewhere nice to celebrate."

Carmen didn't know how Lisa was making her money, but she figured they'd get caught up on all those details once they went out that evening. In other words, she figured Lisa would fill her in on what had really been going on in her life over the past seven years.

"Yeah, I'm sure I don't wanna go anywhere fancy,

Lisa. But I *am* in the mood for a big steak and a twice baked potato. You know anywhere I could get that?"

"I got you, Carmen. There's this place right off of Peachtree. I always go there when I'm in the mood for some real food. I'll pick you up at seven. Is that good?"

"Yep. That'll do."

Lisa made it to Carmen's place a little past seven. Seeing that she was rolling around in a brand-new Mercedes-Benz S class, Carmen figured that her girl was indeed doing something to bring in the big bucks. After giving Lisa a hug, Carmen settled herself into the passenger side seat of her old bestie's whip.

Lisa cracked a smile. "You like my ride, boo?"

Carmen nodded her head in appreciation. "Yeah, girl. It's nice. Real tight."

Carmen wasn't the type of person who got jealous of other people's success, so she wasn't mad at her ex-bestie for being prosperous. However, she couldn't help but wonder what type of occupation would allow her girl to roll around the city in a hundred-thousand dollar car.

"You wanna drive?"

Carmen shook her head. "Naw, boo. My license's expired. Plus I don't have any insurance. I can't get myself caught doing anything that breaks the law. That would mean my butt would be going right back to lock up to finish the two years that are technically left on my sentence."

"Alright. Your call."

Fifteen minutes later, Lisa was pulling up into the parking lot of a restaurant call Red Sizzler. Since they wanted a little privacy to talk, Lisa asked the waitress to give them a booth instead of a regular table. Ten minutes after that, Carmen was sitting down to a big old ribeye and a twice baked potato with a side of chili and salad. Lisa had gotten the same thing. Lisa laughed and said, "This what you were talking about, Carmen?"

Carmen sliced off a piece of steak and dipped it into the little cup of creamed herb butter that had come with it. She nodded her head. "This is sure 'nough what I was talking about. You done hooked a sista up."

For Carmen, sitting there with Lisa was just like old times. "Girl, I could come over here and eat with you like this every day. But I haven't found a job yet. I can't afford it." She frowned. "And once I do find work, I doubt I'll be able to still afford it —," she pointed at her plate, "— according to the menu, this meal right here is thirty bucks."

"Girl, if a job is what you need, you should let me hook you up. You remember Big Ron from the hood, don't you?"

Carmen remembered Big Ron alright. He was her ex J-Dog's number one competitor. She frowned. "You working for Big Ron, Lisa?"

Lisa nodded her head. "Yep. I'm also his part-time girlfriend. That's how I'm able to drive around in that whip we rolled up here in. Big Ron keeps me in the finest clothes. He always looking for fly chicks to bartend or hold down the gambling tables in the back room of the private club he owns — it's down on the south side. That's what I was doing when I started working for him...I was helping handle the poker table."

She smiled and continued speaking. "Big Ron don't too much run drugs anymore — gambling is more of his hustle. And he makes big bucks at it, too. I'm talking about millions of dollars per year. He even has a yacht that he takes people out on for special gambling trips. The yacht is for the big ballers, not them round-the-way hood cats." Her eyes met Carmen's. "So, you want me to help you get that paper, girl?"

The booth that they were sitting in had ceiling-high backs to the booth benches, so Carmen didn't realize that Mr. Pittman had been sitting in the booth adjacent to theirs for the last ten minutes or so. Therefore, she was surprised when he stood up and was standing there by their table.

"Evening, ladies. Good food that they have here, huh?"

Carmen grinned. So did Lisa. "Hey there, Mr. Pittman," Lisa said. "You used to be my favorite teacher. How's life treating you?"

Mr. Pittman didn't let his smile drop. "Life's treating me pretty good. I can't complain. What about yourself?"

"It's all good. Just bringing my girl Carmen here out to dinner. They finally let her out from under them trumped up charges they had against her."

Carmen hadn't told Lisa yet about her having run into Mr. Pittman earlier in the previous day. She'd been meaning to get around to it, but the topic hadn't come up.

Mr. Pittman nodded his head. "I don't mean to be interrupting the two of you lady's meal." His eyes met Carmen's. "But I'd like to have a word with you for a few minutes in private, Miss Flood." He smiled again. "I won't take up too much of your time. I promise."

Carmen had no idea what her old teacher wanted to talk to her about. Out of respect, she nodded her head at the man, smiled, and said, "Sure."

They went outside of the restaurant and found a secluded spot under a tree.

"Okay, Mr. Pittman. What did you need to talk to me about in private?"

He came right out with it. "Yeah... What I wanted to

talk to you about..." He frowned then he said, "I know you and Lisa used to be best friends, but I don't think it's a good idea for you to hang out too tight with her. I wouldn't even be saying anything, but God put it on my heart to step over to your table and tell you that."

Yep, she was frowning by this time, too.

He continued speaking. "I know Lisa's a decent person, but the type of lifestyle she's living is subject to pull you into trouble. You're trying to go somewhere with your life, Carmen. The people you surround yourself with should reflect that. Plus, I'm sure the terms of your release require you to keep your nose out of trouble." His frown deepened. He shook his head again. "Like I said, I know it's not my place to be saying anything, but God put all of that on my heart. I consider myself to be a man of faith, so I try to do what God tells me to do."

"Alright, Mr. Pittman. I'll make a note that you told me all of that... Alright? Now if you'd excuse me, my dinner's getting cold."

As he watched his ex-student's retreating back, part of Kevin felt bad. But a bigger part of him was happy that he'd followed through with the message God had put in his spirit as he'd sat there alone in his booth eating his own dinner. He hadn't been eavesdropping on the two ladies' conversation, no not at all. They'd been speaking loud enough that he hadn't been able to *not* overhear them.

"I hope she heeds your warning, Lord. Hanging out too much with Lisa Carter ain't gonna be nothing but trouble for Carmen."

As soon as Carmen sat back down at the table, Lisa laughed and asked her, "Mr. Pittman wasn't trying to get a hook-up from you was he, boo? He fine and all, so I know he pulling the women. But you know even some of them fine niggas be thirsty."

Carmen had no intentions of letting on to Lisa what their little conversation had been about. She didn't feel like alienating her girl. So she simply smiled, shook her head, and replied, "Naw, boo. Mr. Pittman wasn't hitting on me. He was just giving me some advice on surviving out here on the outside."

"Oh. That was nice of him."

Carmen took a sip of her iced tea. "Yeah, it was nice alright."

The two women stayed there eating dinner for the next twenty minutes or so. Then they left the restaurant.

As Lisa's Mercedes-Benz hit the interstate, she looked over at Carmen in the passenger-side seat and said, "Big Ron is over at his club right now... At least let me drive you over there so you can see how everything is running. I know you said you weren't interested in the job, but once you check out the environment, you might just change your mind. When I was doing the poker table, I was bringing in at least

$1500 a week. I'm sure wherever you been putting in applications, they ain't gonna pay you that much. Shit, your butt'll be lucky if you brought home fifteen hundred in a whole month."

Carmen knew what her girl was telling her was true. When she'd gone to some of the jobs to put in applications that day, she'd actually been quoted some starting salaries. The highest was $10.50 per hour. At forty hours per week, she'd be lucky to bring home thirteen hundred dollars in a month. Let alone fifteen hundred. Fifteen hundred was totally out of the question. "Fifteen-hundred dollars per week, Lisa?"

Lisa nodded her head. "Yeah. $1500 per week... $6000 per month." She laughed. "And it's all under the table, so no taxes."

Carmen sighed. "Okay, boo. I guess it wouldn't hurt to drop by there so I can take a look."

An hour later, Carmen had Mr. Pittman's last words to her on her mind. She couldn't get them out of her head: *You're trying to go somewhere with your life, Carmen. The people you surround yourself with should reflect that. Plus, I'm sure the terms of your release require you to keep your nose out of trouble.*

The more she reflected on all of that, the more she came to realize that the gambling club wasn't the type of environment that she wanted to be working in. She was trying to live a saved lifestyle and everything that club represented was totally against that. Excessive drinking, drugging, swearing, and some of everything else under the sun...you name it it was going on. *I want the money, but this isn't the environment for me, Lord.*

Lisa was grinning from ear to ear. She was right at home. As slot machines sounded in the background, she asked Carmen, "What you think, boo?"

Carmen shook her head. "I can't do this, Lisa. Thanks but no thanks, honey."

Lisa was confused. She'd thought for sure that once she got her homegirl up in the club, she'd be changing her mind. "Are you sure, Carmen?"

Carmen nodded her head. "Yeah. I'm ready to go back to Halo House."

"Well, can you hang around for a couple more hours? One of the girls who work the roulette table just went home sick. Big Ron wants me to take her place for a little while. Her replacement should be here in an an hour or so."

Mr. Pittman's words to her about not spending too much time with Lisa came to Carmen's mind again. *This isn't the place for you, boo*, she thought to herself. *Lisa got you up in here around a lot of mess.*

Carmen shook her head. "You don't have to take me back to the halfway house. I can find my way home. Okay?"

"Alright. See you later."

The halfway house was a good hour's walk away from the club that Carmen was in. Since she didn't know anybody in there, she knew she was gonna be hoofing it. *Well, at least till I get to the next bus stop.* There wasn't anyway she could afford a cab.

She'd only been walking a good minute or two when swat teams swarmed the private, secluded, upscale club that she'd just come out of. She didn't know what was going down, but she was glad that she wasn't up in there. The last place she needed to be was somewhere where illegal activity was going on. That would've been a sure-fire ticket back to prison for her. And she was pretty much sure that the gambling operations inside that club were all illegal.

She still had love in her heart for Lisa, so she said a quick prayer for her girl. There was nothing that she could do for her ex-bestie besides pray, so she picked up her pace and made her way outta dodge.

It took her about an hour to make it home. She'd walked part of the way and taken the city bus for the rest of it. Instead of going inside, she decided to take a seat on the swing that was in a corner of the spacious porch. It was such a beautiful night, that she wanted to stay out there a little longer and enjoy more of it. After all, she hadn't gotten to have such nights while she'd been in lock up.

"Lord," she whispered under her breath. "Thank

45

you for sending Mr. Pittman my way. If I'd stayed up in that club, there's a good chance I would've been right where I came from yesterday right now. But you didn't let that happen to me. You kept me."

She'd been mad at her old teacher earlier that evening when he'd first told her about how hanging out with Lisa was a bad idea. Every last one of those bad feelings had disappeared now. They'd gone poof like smoke.

As she was sitting out there in that porch swing, a newer model Ford truck — an F-350 — pulled up into the halfway house's driveway. Despite herself, her heart went pitter-patter when Mr. Pittman stepped out of the vehicle and made his way over to the front steps. *Lord that man really is fine*, she couldn't help but think to herself. A little under six feet, with a solid muscular body, and a chocolate-colored face that looked like it belonged in Hollywood or somewhere. Yep, he was definitely a ten plus in the looks department in Carmen's book.

"Hey Carmen. Lord knows it's good to see your face just about now."

Carmen was confused. She'd just seen Mr. Pittman a little over two hours ago. *Why is he looking so happy to see me now?*

He cleared all of that up in his next statement. "I just got finished watching part of the ten o'clock news—," he frowned. "The police just busted up an

46

upscale, illegal gambling operation. I saw them arresting Lisa and Big Ron on the TV screen." He shook his head. "I was worried about you. I knew you and Lisa had been together tonight. I was hoping you hadn't gotten yourself caught up in all of that mess."

Carmen frowned, too, at this point. She sure felt bad for her girl.

She placed her feet on the wooden floor, thus stopping her swinging motion on the porch swing. "So that's what all the police officers were about." She shook her head. "I was walking away from the club when all of that went down." Her eyes met his. "The minute I walked into that club, I got to thinking about everything you told me back at the restaurant — I couldn't get it out of my mind. Your words kept reverberating in my head, making me realize that that club wasn't the place I needed to be."

She sighed. "Deep down in my heart, in my spirit, I knew I didn't belong there. But it was your words that forced me to take action and leave. You saved me, Mr. Pittman. Thank you for that."

He shook his head. "I'm glad that you got yourself out of there, Carmen. But in all reality, all the thanks goes to God. He's the one who put in my spirit to tell you what I told you."

Carmen was feeling kind of emotional about the whole situation. Because of this, she stood up from the swing and took one of Mr. Pittman's hands into both of hers. Her eyes met his. With a sincere look in them she said, "Thing is, you didn't have to say anything. But you did. You chose to listen to God—," she shook her head, "— we don't all choose to listen when the Lord talks to us. But you did and I sincerely thank you...I thank you from the very bottom of my heart for that."

The sincere look in her dark eyes touched him, too, at that particular moment. "You're welcome, Carmen."

For some reason, they just stood there staring at each other for another four or five seconds. Then Carmen realized that she'd grabbed the man's hand and was still holding on to it. She got a little embarrassed about that. To cover up her action, she smiled and said, "Oh, I guess I'll give you your hand back now."

Mr. Pittman grinned, too. "Yeah, that'll probably be a good idea. Else I won't be able to make it inside to give my Aunt Michelle her slice of strawberry cheesecake. She loves the cheesecake that they serve at the Red Sizzler. Every time I eat dinner there, I bring her over a slice. She was expecting me here a half hour ago with it." He laughed, then continued speaking. "I better get it to her before she puts me over her knee and gives me a spanking."

Carmen laughed, too. She had a hard time imagining the sweet, little Mrs. Ridley putting anybody as big as her full grown nephew over her knee.

"I'll go ahead and leave you to enjoy your night, Carmen."

"Alright, Mr. Pittman. Enjoy the rest of your night, too."

Carmen only stayed out there for another minute or so, then she went inside to her room. A half hour later, she showered and crawled into her single bed. While in prison, it had become her habit to read her Bible before going to sleep each night. She reached over on the nightstand and grabbed her well-worn holy book.

Fifteen minutes later, she finally began saying her prayers for the evening. She wasn't surprised at all that she'd added her girl, Lisa, to her nightly prayer list. However, she was a little bit surprised that she'd also added Mr. Pittman.

After she'd said 'amen', she smiled to herself. *I really shouldn't be surprised that I'm praying for him, too — it's really nothing personal. He's good people and he really had my back tonight. Thank you Lord for sending that man my way. And thank you Mr. Pittman for doing what God had put on your heart to do.*

Across Town:

Mr. Pittman finished saying his nightly prayers and crawled into his king-sized, four-poster bed. He as well had said a little prayer for his ex-student, Lisa. He'd prayed that she'd accept God into her heart so that her life could be put her on the right path. He, of course, hadn't forgotten about Carmen. She'd been on his mind during his entire drive home from the halfway house that evening. He'd had a very different prayer in reference to her. He'd prayed that the powerful God that they served would give her every desire of her heart.

He hadn't been eavesdropping on Lisa and Carmen's conversation at the restaurant. But he'd overheard Carmen telling Lisa about how she'd given a homeless woman the last five dollars that had been in her pocket earlier that day — all because the woman had said that it was her five-year old's birthday and she'd wanted to buy the little boy a slice of cake and a candle. The woman had told Carmen that she didn't have but thirty-two cents to her name. Carmen had given the woman her last.

Mr. Pittman frowned. He knew for a fact that each newly-released felon that entered his aunt and uncle's halfway-house was only given a one-time cash stipend of twenty-five bucks by his auntie and uncle. He was pretty much sure that twenty-five dollars was all that Carmen had had to her name. Yet, with no job at hand, she'd chosen to brighten the young mother and son's day.

He smiled as he closed his eyes. *She's good people, Lord. Beautiful, kind, loving, caring. She deserves a break*.

CHAPTER 4

"Am I ever gonna find a job, Lord?" Those were the words that Carmen had just whispered under her breath as she got off the phone with yet another company informing her that they didn't have a position available for her.

"Still no luck, chica?" Janelle asked as she came out the front door and joined Carmen out on the porch.

Carmen shook her head. "Naw, boo." She sighed. "Another rejection."

"If I had a job, I sure would give it to you, Carmen. You're a good worker. Mr. and Mrs. Ridley has all of us who live here doing chores. But you're one of the few who actually pulls her own weight. Some of these jokers up in here be straight tripping. Mr. and Mrs. Ridley always gotta get on them about doing what they supposed to be doing."

One thing that Carmen believed in for sure was doing her share of the work. She hadn't had a perfect mother, but Gina Flood had definitely instilled a positive work ethic into both of her kids.

Carmen gave Janelle a smile. "That's enough of

listening to my bad news, I hear that somebody got themselves a little promotion on the job."

Janelle grinned right back. "I did indeed. You looking at the new assistant manager at Auto Parts World over on Peachtree."

Still smiling, Carmen stuck her hand high up in the air. "Go ahead and give me a high five on that, boo. That's what I'm talking about right there. God's in the blessing business. I been praying for you on that." She'd been praying for Janelle about some other things too — namely the lesbian lifestyle she was living — but that was a totally different discussion. She wasn't getting into all of that today.

"I told you I could get you on where I work, Carmen."

"Working at Auto Parts World would actually mean I'd have to know something about cars. I can't tell an engine from a carburetor, Janelle. I'm not qualified to work there. But I know God's got something in the works for me.

Janelle couldn't help but wrinkle her eyebrows together in a frown. She took a seat on the porch swing right beside Carmen. "That's something that confuses me, Carmen. You got locked up for only trying to defend yourself. You did seven years in prison. You can't find a job, you really don't have any connections with family, and your best friend just got locked up herself... With all of that going wrong in your life, how come you still running round here talking about God and how he's blessing people."

That statement from her new friend didn't phase Carmen at all. She simply smiled, nodded her head, and said, "That's where faith comes in. I have to believe that even though everything is going wrong in my life right now, it's all part of God's master plan. I may not see the direction that he's trying to lead me in, but my faith lets me know that he is indeed leading me."

Janelle gave that some thought for several seconds. "Faith you say?"

Carmen nodded her head again. "Yeah. Faith."

Janelle picked up her Auto Parts World hat from off of the seat of the porch swing. "Alright, Carmen. I guess I kinda understand all of that. But on a different note, I got a half hour to get downtown to work. I'll catch you on the flipside... Okay, boo?"

"Okay, Janelle. Later."

As Janelle made her way to work, she had everything that she and Carmen had just talked about still on her mind. *Maybe I should give this God that Carmen is talking about a try. It can't hurt nothing.*

Then she glanced over at the dark-chocolate complected girl who was sitting beside her on the city bus. She smiled and shook her head. *Naw, God ain't down with the lesbo thing. I ain't ready to turn down*

54

having my fingers all up in the coochy yet. She gave the girl in the seat beside her a little smile. Then she winked her eye. "Hey, boo. That's a pretty dress you got on. It sure do bring out your shape real nice."

<<<<<>>>>>

Later on that Night at Halo House:

Carmen was convinced that the porch swing at her new digs was her favorite piece of furniture in the whole wide world. If she wasn't job hunting or doing chores around the house, she was out there on that porch swing. The sun had set fifteen minutes ago and sitting there is where she was. She recognized Mr. Pittman's truck, so she knew it was his vehicle that had just pulled into the driveway.

"Hey, Carmen. What you doing out here by yourself in the dark?" He smiled after he'd made his comment.

Despite her job problems, Carmen smiled, too. "Just out here trying to enjoy the night a little bit. What brings you back over here at almost nine o'clock in the evening."

Mr. Pittman hadn't seen Carmen in a whole two weeks, but she'd still been on his mind. He'd come over to drop off another slice of cheesecake for his auntie. But truth be told, he'd gone to Red Sizzler to get the dessert all because he'd wanted an excuse to see Carmen again. He hadn't been able to get her off of his mind, so he was trying to see if thinking about her like that was just a fluke or something. She was no longer the young girl that he'd had in his twelfth grade Civics class. She was an attractive woman who he'd come to realize had piqued his interest.

Carmen noticed the bag from Red Sizzler in his hand almost as soon as the words had come out of her mouth, inquiring on his reason for being there. "Oh, you're bringing Mrs. Ridley another slice of that cheesecake. You sure are a good nephew."

"I try to be. Like I told you a few weeks ago, she's good to me, so I can't help but be good to her."

Carmen was a little nervous sitting out there talking to Mr. Pitman like she was doing — even though she knew she really didn't have a reason to be. Then the little voice in her head said: *The reason why your butt is nervous is because you're attracted to him. Yep, that's right... You're attracted to him, boo. You got the hots for his fine behind.*

Carmen knew for a fact that her ex-teacher was gonna think she was crazy if she told the voice out loud to be quiet. But that's exactly what she felt like doing.

Mr. Pittman continued speaking. "It's a nice evening. I really don't blame you for wanting to be outside." He smiled. "My aunt and uncle have owned this house ever since I was little. I used to sleep over a lot of nights in the summer. And I sure did spend my fair share of time out here on that there porch swing." He chuckled. "I've repaired it my fair share of times, too."

Carmen laughed. "You over there sounding all nostalgic and everything. You making me think you wanna sit down and swing for a spell." She shrugged her shoulders. "I don't mind the company if that's what you're wanting to do."

He wasn't about to turn her invitation down. *After all*, he thought to himself, *it's only an invitation to share this swing for a little while. She's nice like that. She's not trying to push up on me or anything* — even though part of him was wishing that she was.

They sat out there shooting the breeze for almost an hour. They weren't talking about anything in particular, but by the time Carmen stood up and told him it was well past her bedtime, she felt like they'd been out there for an eternity — a very good eternity.

Mr. Pittman stood as well. "I hope my aunt hasn't gone to bed yet."

Carmen laughed. "I'm sure Mrs. Ridley is gonna have time for her Knee-Knee dropping by. Especially since he's bringing over her favorite dessert."

Mr. Pittman grinned, too. His aunt still occasionally called him the nickname from his youth. Not often. But enough times that Carmen had picked up on it in the short three weeks that she'd been at Halo House.

He held the front door open so that Carmen could enter before him. Needless to say, she felt special from his little act of chivalry. She'd never had a man or boy get a door for her like that. That hadn't exactly been the type of people she'd had in her life growing up. And it certainly hadn't been the case in prison — where she'd currently spent the majority of her adult years.

"Good night, Carmen. I'll see you later...okay?"

She gave him a shy little smile. "Okay, Mr. Pittman. By the way, I think I hear your auntie in the kitchen."

Less than thirty seconds later, Kevin was in the kitchen with his Aunt Michelle.

Michelle took a seat at her kitchen table and sunk her fork into her slice of silky cheesecake. "You sure are spoiling me, nephew."

"Just trying to keep that pretty smile on my favorite auntie's face."

Michelle kept on eating her cheesecake. Without looking her nephew in the eye she replied, "From the look of things this evening, it seemed like to me you were trying to keep a smile on that pretty little thing, Carmen's, face too."

He didn't say anything in response to that. However, his auntie laughed and added, "I actually like Carmen. She may have gotten herself into trouble as a kid — locked up for what she did defending herself — but she's good people. I can tell the ones with good hearts. And she's definitely one of those." Michelle nodded her head. "God's got his hand of protection over the rest of that girl's life. She's going some good places, Kevin. Mark my word. You just wait and see." She winked her eye. "I can definitely tell why you've taken a liking to her."

"Who's to say I've taken a liking to her Aunt Michelle?"

"Boy, please. I changed your diapers. I've been knowing your butt ever since you was knee-high to a grasshopper. I know when my Knee-Knee got the hots for somebody."

At that point, Kevin didn't feel like denying it. It was his attraction to Carmen that had him up in his aunt's kitchen that very evening. Other than that, he would've been home in bed getting some precious shut eye.

"You intend on asking her out anytime soon? Or do you intend on waiting until she gets her life together a little bit more?"

Kevin smiled. He stood up from his perch on a barstool at the kitchen island. Then he walked over and put a loving kiss on his auntie's cheek. "See you later, Aunt Michelle. I think I'll head on home now."

Michell knew she'd called it right where Kevin's attraction to Carmen was concerned. "Don't wait too long, Kevin. Carmen is a fine woman. There's gonna be plenty of men waiting to snatch her right on up.

You don't wanna get yourself caught slipping. You know...since you're interested and whatnot."

During his entire fifteen minute drive back home, Kevin had his aunt's parting words on his mind. *Aunt Michelle is probably right. Carmen's a catch. She's down on her luck right now. But soon enough she's gonna be on her A-game. I want to be the man she stepping with when she gets there... Shoot 'before' she gets there.*

As he made his way into his two-story home in the suburbs, he made up his mind that he intended to not only get to know the grown-up version of Carmen a little better, he also intended to woo her. He grinned to himself. *And I know exactly how Imma start going about all of that.*

The Following Morning:

Kevin purposely walk into his office at Pondfield Preparatory Academy an hour early. He had to get a jumpstart on the plan that had formed in his mind the previous evening.

He booted up his computer and immediately got started on the proposal for the administrators of the school. A half hour later, he had a wide smile on his face as he sent an email to the correct recipients.

"That should do it right there. The wheels are in motion now."

It took a short four hours for him to get the response back from his email that he was hoping for. He grinned to himself. The chief administrator of the school where he worked had approved his request. *I can't wait to talk to Carmen.*

<<<<<>>>>>

Once again, Carmen had spent her entire morning job searching. Needless to say, she was tired when she made it back to Halo House that afternoon.

She went straight to her room and flopped down on her bed. She'd only been in there a minute or so when there was a knocking sound at her door.

She stood up to go answer it. She smiled when she pulled the door open and found Janelle standing on the other side.

"Hey, Carmen. Mrs. Ridley baked a couple apple pies this morning while you were gone." She handed Carmen a Tupperware container. "I snagged two slices for you...you know, before these greedy MFer's round here ate it all."

Carmen gratefully took the desserts from Janelle's hand. "Thank you, girl. You must've known the type of morning I had. Something sweet would sure hit the spot just about now." She frowned. "I've been putting in job applications everywhere, but nobody's biting. I'm gonna have to move up out of here if I can't find a job."

Janelle shook her head. "Naw, boo. Mr. and Mrs. Ridley ain't gonna evict you since you trying. They're nice like that — plus they like you." Janelle couldn't help but skim her eyes over Carmen real quick from head to toe. She smiled. "I like you, too. If you were my woman, you wouldn't even have to worry about having a job. I'd be paying your rent here for you."

To that, Carmen laughed. "You know I don't roll like that, Janelle. Girl, I'm keeping your butt under prayer."

"See, Carmen... That's what I like about you. You're strong in your faith and your belief in God, but you don't look down your nose at me because of the lifestyle I'm living."

Carmen shook her head. "Judging someone because they're homosexual isn't my job. Now I'm gonna be upfront with you: I don't approve of homosexualism. But that's between you and God. As far as I see it, I'm supposed to treat people right — show them love — despite all of that."

Carmen paused for a moment then said, "Speaking of showing love — the Bible even says that folks are supposed to show love toward each other. If you're interested in reading about it yourself, it's in the book of John...Chapter 13, Verse 30. Now I'm not gonna try to misrepresent things — because the Bible does indeed say that homosexuality is a sinful act. There's other sinful acts in the Bible, too. Like lying, stealing, killing, committing adultery...they're all sins in God's eyes. It ain't up to me to judge."

Janelle laughed. "You ever think of becoming a preacher, Carmen? I think you'd be good at that."

Carmen smiled. "Nope. Never. Since I think you got my message, I think I'll go ahead and step down from my little soapbox."

Janelle actually appreciated the word that Carmen was dropping down on her. Janelle's family was full of regular churchgoers — even a couple of pastors. All of them had rejected her because she was a lesbian. Carmen was the only Christian she'd run into who actually seemed to be interested in showing her some unconditional love — without stepping away from her religious convictions, of course. Janelle appreciated her new friend for all of that.

"When you go to church this Sunday, Carmen...do you mind if I tag along?"

Carmen smiled from ear to ear. "Of course not, boo. Come right along."

Janelle grinned, too. Then she nodded her head. "Enjoy your dessert and you free time today, chica. I need to cut on out of here and get to work."

Carmen spent the rest of the day helping Mrs. Ridley with chores around the house. Mrs. Ridley was sitting in the study with her husband catching The Family Feud when Carmen finished scrubbing down the three bathrooms in Halo House. Mrs. Ridley hadn't asked her to do it, she'd volunteered.

"I took care of the bathrooms for you today, Mrs. Ridley. Is there anything else you need me to do before I wind down and go relax out there on the front porch?"

Mrs. Ridley shook her head. "Naw, baby. You did more than your fair share of helping me out around here today."

"It's the least I can do, Mrs. Ridley. I haven't been able to pay you guys one red cent since I got here. And I been here a whole three weeks…going on four."

"Like I told you a few days ago… Don't worry yourself about that, chile. You're gonna find a job, and then you're gonna be able to start paying."

Carmen sure was happy about the faith that Mrs. Ridley had in that happening for her. She was ashamed to admit it, but her faith was beginning to dwindle to nothing in that particular area of her life.

"Like I said…don't you worry about yourself about finding a job, Carmen. It'll come. Alright?"

Carmen smiled. She nodded her head. "I'm sure it will, Mrs. Ridley. I'm about to step out on the porch… Okay?"

"Alright, baby."

When Mr. Pittman rolled up, Carmen had been

sitting out on the porch swing for only a few minutes. As soon as he stepped foot on the porch she smiled and said, "What...no cheesecake for your auntie this evening?"

He shook his head. "Nope. I actually dropped by today to talk to you."

Yep, he'd piqued her interest. "Talk to me?"

He nodded. "Yeah." He pointed at the porch swing. "Mind if I sit down?"

"Sure, sure...have a seat."

Kevin didn't know what perfume Carmen used, but he loved the scent that always seemed to be associated with her. It was a light, summery smell — very feminine...kinda like honeysuckles and lemon — and he enjoyed it.

"What's up, Mr. Pittman?"

He leaped right into the conversation at hand. "I understand from my Aunt Michelle that you're still looking for a job."

Carmen got excited. "Yeah. I am." Her eyes met his. "You know somebody who's hiring a reformed ex-felon with excellent people skills?"

He smiled. "Actually I do. Me."

She didn't understand what he was talking about. "You?" she asked, nearly in disbelief.

"Yes. Me. The last time we talked, I told you that I was no longer teaching at McKinley. I'm now a vice principal at a private school — it's call Pondfield Preparatory Academy. Well, Pondfield has had the option to hire an executive assistant for the vice principals for a year or so. I talked to the administrators today. The jobs yours if you want it."

Heck yeah she wanted it. She got excited over everything that Mr. Pittman had just told her. Then her feelings of excitement crashed. "I'm an ex-felon. Nobody is gonna want someone like myself working at a school. Isn't it against the law in Georgia?"

He smiled. "Since you're the lawyer-to-be, technically, you're right. However, that only applies to public schools. Pondfield is a private institution. And yes, I told them about your incarceration. But since I'm willing to vouch for your character, they're willing to take you on."

Carmen was beyond excited now. She took both of Mr. Pittman's hands into hers. "Lord, Mr. Pittman, you don't know how happy of a woman you just made me. I could kiss your fine self right here and now."

Kevin really was attracted to Carmen, so he wasn't averse to her kissing him. And he liked the fact that she'd just called him 'fine'.

Realizing what she'd just said, her cheeks heated in embarrassment. She frowned. Then she gave him a sheepish little smile. "Sorry about that, Mr. Pittman. I got a little bit too excited."

He laughed. "Well, it's definitely good to know that I still got it. I'm pushing thirty-five now. A brotha my age likes to hear that a beautiful young lady like yourself thinks he's fine. You did say I'm fine... Didn't you?"

She'd said it alright. Now she didn't know what to say to him in response.

He took all that worry away from her with his next statement. He laughed again and said, "You don't even have to answer that. I understand that it was the excitement from finally having a job. Can you come in tomorrow morning and officially fill out your paperwork?"

She nodded her head. "Yep. I can definitely do that."

"I can pick you up if you need me to. Halo House is right in between my home and Pondfield Academy. It wouldn't be any trouble to me at all."

Having a ride directly there sure would beat having to take two or three buses. "You sure about that, Mr. Pittman?"

"Yep. I'm positive. I got your back. I'll be rolling through here at eight. Cool?"

She nodded her head. "Yep."

CHAPTER 5

Carmen could tell that she was definitely going to like her job working at Pondfield Academy. The place basically catered to middle-classed African-American and Latino-American families. But it was run very professionally, while having a laid-back, fun type of atmosphere. It was nothing like the schools in the heart of the hood that Carmen had attended.

The only problem she foresaw herself having was clothes. Most of the stuff that Mrs. Ridley had handed down to her was casualwear. She had a couple of dresses, but that was just about it.

Mr. Pittman wrapped up the tour of the facility that he'd just been giving his newest employee. "Well, Carmen. You think you're gonna like it here?"

She nodded her head. "Yep. I'm sure I am."

"Well, what's the problem. I can see that something's bothering you."

They were alone in his office by this time. She was ashamed of admitting what the problem was. She forced herself to smile. "There's no problem, Mr. Pittman. I'm just grateful to have this job. I feel like the most blessed woman on God's green Earth."

He reached into a folder in his desk and pulled out a check. He handed it to Carmen. "The school normally only gives sign-on bonuses to administrators and whatnot. But I was able to convince them to make an exception in your case."

She looked down at the check that he'd just handed her. It was for a thousand dollars. It was more than enough to buy some clothes that were appropriate for work and then some. She knew of some discount stores where she could get some quality threads while stretching her dollar at the same time. Her forced smile became genuine. It even lit up her eyes. "Lord have mercy, thank you, Mr. Pittman. You're a lifesaver."

"You deserve to catch a break, Carmen. Now I know this is kinda last minute, but do you wanna go out to Red Sizzler this evening to celebrate?"

"Sure. Why not? But you're gonna have to promise me that you'll let me buy Mrs. Ridley's slice of strawberry cheesecake this go around. I owe her for how good she's been to me. Your uncle, too. By the way, what do you think I can do for him?"

Mr. Pittman laughed. "Unc's a Falcons fan. Any type of Atlanta Falcon paraphernalia would be a good gift for him."

Carmen smiled. "I'm on it. But I'm gonna have to buy Mrs. Ridley a whole cheesecake to be fair."

"I hear cheesecakes freeze real good. I'm sure she'll appreciate you for buying it for her."

Since she wasn't going to be starting her first day of work until Monday — which was almost a whole week away — Carmen decided to cash her sign-on bonus check right after leaving Pondfield Academy that morning. Mr. Pittman had offered to drive her into town, but she felt like he'd done enough for her already. Plus, he had a full day of work ahead of him. Therefore, she turned down his offer of a ride. She walked to the closest bus stop and went from there instead.

She understood that she and her new boss weren't going out on a real date. But that didn't mean she didn't intend on looking nice for their dinner appointment. In her eyes, she was still broke. So she decided to go to a thrift store to find something nice to wear to dinner that evening.

She made it back to Halo House around one thirty that afternoon, which would give her plenty of time to get ready for being picked up at 6 o'clock by Mr. Pittman.

"Lord, chile. It looks like somebody's been shopping today."

Carmen was all smiles. "You're not gonna believe it, Mrs. Ridley. I got myself a job. Not only that, but I also got a thousand dollar sign-on bonus. I'll be able to pay you your four hundred dollars for this month's rent as soon as my money clears the bank tomorrow."

"That's wonderful news, Carmen. I told you something would come along. Didn't I?"

A knowing look came on Carmen's pretty face. She was sure that Mrs. Ridley had talked to her nephew about giving her a job. "You didn't have anything to do with me getting hired, now did you, Mrs. Ridley?"

"It depends on who gave you a job, baby. I put in a good word for you at a lot of places."

"It was your nephew, Kevin. I mean Mr. Pittman. I'm gonna be his assistant over at Pondfield Academy."

Mrs. Ridley shook her head. "That was all my nephew's doing. I didn't even know they had a position open over there."

"Well, it sure was a Godsend. I can tell you that much."

Mrs. Ridley wasn't telling Carmen, but she suspected that her nephew had pulled the position out of thin air for the young lady he was interested in. She'd known men to do stranger things to help out women they were falling for.

"Yep. I agree with you Carmen. Getting a job like that out of the blue is indeed a Godsend." She pointed at the shopping bags. "I guess the bags are your new work clothes… Huh?"

Carmen frowned. She didn't know exactly what to

say, because she didn't know how Mrs. Ridley was going to feel about her nephew taking a girl who was an ex-felon out to dinner. She finally responded with, "I did indeed buy some clothes for work today, some other things, too."

"You should probably let me make you a special dinner this evening to celebrate. You know I love cooking."

"Um… Well…"

"You have other plans. That's what it is."

Since Mr. Pittman was going to be picking her up from Halo House that evening, Carmen figured she might as well just come on out with it. "Yeah, I actually do have plans this evening. Your nephew thought it would be a good idea if he bought me dinner to celebrate. You know how nice he is and all. According to him, you practically helped raise him. So I know you know what a big heart he got."

A knowing smile came on Mrs. Ridley's face. "I'm okay with you going out with Kevin, Carmen. You're good people. A body can't have too many good people in their life — my nephew included."

Carmen shook her head. "It's not a real date, Mrs. Ridley. So don't worry. Kevin's not trying to hook up with a felon like myself."

"I've known non-felons who have a whole lot less morals than you, Carmen. Don't keep berating yourself, girl. You good people and you got a good heart." She pointed at Carmen's head. "You know I'm good at doing hair, don't you? Let me hook you up with a cute little perm rod set for your special celebratory night out on the town. That sound good to you?"

Carmen was all for that. "Would you, Mrs. Ridley?"

"Of course, chile. Meet me down in the basement in a half hour. Alright?"

"Alright."

Three and a half hours later, as Carmen stood in front of the mirror in her room staring at her reflection, she knew her look was on point. Mrs. Ridley had slayed her head. She had a perfect halo of curls that made her look like a chocolate angel. And the dress she was rocking was cute in a sophisticated, fun type of way.

She stepped out of her room intending on making it down to the front porch swing to wait for her date. Before she could make it to her destination, she was stopped by Janelle.

"Damn, Carmen. I knew you were cute when you first walked up in here. But when you lay it down like that —," she eyed Carmen from head to toe, "— you make a lesbo sista like myself wanna turn a blind eye on all the other beautiful females in the room."

Carmen smiled at her friend. Then she laughed. "You need to quit, Janelle."

Janelle let out a low whistle. "I'm just telling you the truth, baby girl. Whoever you going out with this evening is lucky as hell." She smiled. "You gonna break him off a little something something?"

"Girl, you know I told your butt that I'm celibate. I ain't giving up the goodies to nobody unless they got a ring on it. Anyways, it ain't like I'm going out on a real date. I got offered a job today and my new boss is taking me out to dinner at The Red Sizzler to celebrate. So it's a business dinner. Not pleasure."

"When I got hired on at the Auto Parts World, didn't nobody offer to take my ass out to dinner. Where you get a job at, Carmen, that they taking you out to eat to celebrate?"

"I got hired on at Pondfield Academy as an executive assistant."

"That sounds fancy."

"Not really. I'm just gonna be a glorified secretary to the vice principal staff over there."

All of that sounded familiar to Janelle for some reason. She suddenly snapped her fingers. "Wait a minute. Ain't that the school that Mrs. Ridley's nephew works at? He's a Vice Principal over there... Right?"

"Yeah. He's the one who hired me."

"He trying to push up on the kitty cat, boo."

Carmen shook her head. "Girl. That man ain't trying to push up on nothing that I got. He's just being nice."

"Now I know you not stupid, Carmen. So you must just be slow. Ain't no man gonna take a woman out to a restaurant where it's thirty-five dollars a plate just because he's nice. At least not no black man."

"Saved and godly men like Mr. Pittman do. Besides...you've seen him. He's a catch. He can have any woman that he wants. Why in the world would he want to come deal with somebody like myself on a romantic level?"

"You must not realize that you're a catch, Carmen. You still thinking like an inmate. You back in the real world, boo. You on the outside, and you got a lot going for yourself. You gorgeous and you about to be a lawyer. And you nice, too. I don't know any man in his right mind who wouldn't want to be with a girl like you." Janelle didn't know many lesbian women either who wouldn't want to be with Carmen. She sure knew that she'd wanted her when she'd first moved into Halo House almost a month ago. *Shoot, I'd get with her fine ass right now if she would let me.*

"It's almost six, Janelle. My dinner ticket for the evening will be here any minute. I'll see you later. Okay?"

"Okay, Carmen."

Another resident at the house, Jarrod, smiled at Carmen as she walked downstairs. Jarrod and Carmen were about the same age — twenty-five. He'd had a thing for Carmen since the day she'd moved into Halo

House, just like Janelle had. He smiled and began flirting like he usually did with Carmen. "Damn, girl. You pretty every day, but you killing 'em tonight. You stepping out on Jesus and going to the club?"

Carmen and Jarrod always kidded around with each other. He reminded her a whole lot of her little brother.

Carmen laughed. "Nope. Me and JC still tight. And thanks I think for the compliment, Jarrod. I got myself a job. I'm just going out to celebrate."

"Good for you, baby girl."

When Jarrod got to the top of the stairs he smiled at Janelle who was still standing there. "I bet you was hoping that she'd dressed up like that for you, won't you, Janelle?"

Jarrod didn't like lesbians, and Janelle knew that. She frowned at him. "Boy, shut your mouth before I pop you in it."

"Keep talking to me like that, Janelle, and you're gonna make me think that you want me to lay some of this pipe right here up in you." He grabbed his crotch so that Janelle would know exactly what he was talking about.

Janelle shook her head. "I got to see exactly what you're working with when you came out the shower last week and dropped your towel on the accident tip. Even if I wasn't gay, it would take more than three little inches to satisfy a girl like me. In fact, non-packing men like yourself is probably the reason why I crossed over to the other side. Now ruminate on that for a little while. I got things I need to be taking care of."

With that being said, Janelle disappeared into her own room. *I can't stand Jarrod ass.*

Out on the front porch, Carmen ended up not waiting for Mr. Pittman on the porch swing like she'd intended. That's because he drove up the second she stepped foot out there.

He got the car door for her, then came and settled himself behind the steering wheel of a fully-loaded BMW.

The only vehicle Carmen had ever seen Mr. Pittman driving had been his newer model Ford F-350 truck. She ran her hand over the soft leather of the center console of the ride. "This is nice, Mr. Pittman. You borrowed it from somebody?"

He smiled. He shook his head. "Naw. I'm a casual type of brotha at heart, so I prefer driving my truck most of the time. I only take my baby out on the town for special occasions, and for church on Sundays."

Is he trying to say that taking me out to dinner to celebrate me getting a job is a special occasion? She certainly hoped so. Because in her eyes, everybody deserved to feel special — at least every now or then.

He merged with the traffic on the interstate. "And before you ask... Yes, taking you out to dinner this evening is a special occasion in my eyes."

She suddenly felt shy. "Oh."

"And since I failed to say anything before we took off, let me go ahead and tell you that you look lovely this evening...absolutely stunning. I'm gonna have the finest woman in the restaurant on my arm tonight."

She actually knew how to take a compliment so she said, "Thank you, Mr. Pittman. I can't take all the credit for my looks this evening, though. Your auntie hooked my hair up. Instead of tending to a halfway house, she should have a salon somewhere."

"Yeah. She used to have a booth in a salon in her younger days. Then she got tired of what she called 'drama' that was going on in whatever salon she'd worked at."

Carmen understood exactly what he was talking about. "Anytime you have multiple personalities in one confined environment, drama is gonna show up. It's not a matter of '*if*' it'll show up, it's a matter of '*when*'." She frowned. "That's one of the very first things I learned from my time in lockup."

He nodded his head in understanding. If he'd had the ability to take those seven years she'd done away, he would've in a heartbeat. "Did you keep a journal, Carmen?"

"Yeah, I kept a journal. It was part of my JJs. My JJs was the only thing that kept me sane."

"Your JJs?"

She finally lifted her lips in a tiny smile again. "Yeah. My JJ'. My Journal and my Jesus. Both of them kept me sane in the midst of all the craziness that was going on all around me."

"You know you're a strong woman, don't you, Carmen?"

"I didn't tend to look at it like that. I tended to think that I was just surviving."

He reached over and gave her hand a squeeze. "You're strong. Trust and believe that. You got locked up at seventeen — you were still a child. But you thrived."

Yeah, it felt weird having him hold her hand like he'd just done. But it was a good kind of weird. A kind that she actually enjoyed.

He continued speaking. "You didn't allow prison to kill your spirit like I've seen happen with a lot of people. It didn't rob you of your joy."

She had a look of doubt written all over her face when she glanced over at him.

As if reading her mind he said, "I didn't exactly have a silver spoon in my mouth while I was growing up. Life was a challenge. My mother was a single parent. Unfortunately, she turned to drugs and alcohol in her attempts to drown out the pain of the type of lifestyle that we were living. That's why I ended up spending a lot of time with my uncle and auntie. I rose up from the streets into the man I am today. I've seen a lot of people close to me go down during the journey. People making bad choices, bad decisions."

He glanced over and his eyes met hers. "Can you believe I spent three years as a teenager in juvie? My sister — who's only a year older than me — she was dating this dude who was twenty-one. I was fourteen, my sister was fifteen. He wanted to put his hands on her, so I stabbed him. I'm not proud of it, but I took a life. Fortunately, I wasn't tried as an adult like you were. The prosecutors looked at the extenuating circumstances. They let me out of lockdown when I turned eighteen. The court sealed my records and I was able to move on with my life. I moved in with my aunt and uncle — I think my experience had a lot to do with them wanting to open a halfway house for ex-cons. They convinced me to go to college. And here I am, as a thirty-four year old man. I'm changed and living a life on the right path."

Carmen never would've guessed all of that about the man sitting beside her. She shook her head. "I guess we have something in common."

"Yeah. We do. That's why I keep telling you that you can still build a decent life for yourself. You don't have to be forever bound by what you did."

Carmen knew from that point forward that she had a different type of respect for Kevin Pittman. Yeah, she had respected him before, but she respected him even more now.

"Looks can be deceiving, can't they?" he asked.

"Yeah. I guess so."

<<<<<>>>>>

Carmen couldn't remember the last time she'd had such an enjoyable evening. She had the very same  dinner that she'd had the day she and Lisa had gone to Red Sizzler, but Kevin had insisted that she have a lobster tail to go with her steak, baked potato, and salad. The lobster tail added an additional twenty-five dollars to her already thirty-five dollar plate.

She'd told her date that she didn't need the addition — even though she'd secretly wanted it. He'd insisted that she give it a try. So she had.

Carmen was full in a good kind of way when she walked out of there. She'd had so much food that she decided to take half of it home with her in a doggy bag.

As they hit the interstate on their way back to Halo House, Kevin asked, "Did you have a good time this evening, Carmen?"

She smiled. She nodded her head. "Yeah. I did. Thank you for taking me out to celebrate my new job, boss. And by the way, congratulations on making principal. You came a long ways from being a Civics and Economics teacher over at McKinley. It's a nice accomplishment."

He laughed. "You angling for another date, Carmen. Cause if you are, flattery just might get you anything from me," he kidded.

"It's a good thing I know you're joking, Mr. Pittman."

"But on the serious tip, though. I have tickets to the GospelFest that's being held next weekend. Wanna go?"

"Are you for real?"

"Yep."

She got excited. "Just as long as you can get me back home by your aunt and uncle's curfew, I'm all for it. I heard about the event in church a couple weeks ago. Seeing that I didn't have a job at the time, I pretty much figured I wasn't gonna be able to go. I couldn't afford a ticket."

He smiled. "Look at God...right? Not only are you going to the concert, but you got a job, too. You're a regular ol' Cinderella from the hood aren't you?"

She laughed. "Yep. And you're my Fairy Godfather."

"Fairy Godfather?"

"Yeah."

He got out of the car and escorted Carmen to the front door of Halo House. He wanted to kiss her as they stood out there on that front porch saying their goodnights. But he knew it was much too early in the game for all of that. *Just play it cool, ol' man*, he thought to himself. *She's liking you. You don't want to be too aggressive and scare her off. Give her some time to smell you...to get used to you.*

He smiled. "Good night, Cinderella. Thank you for sharing your evening with me."

She grinned right back. "Good night, Mr. Pittman. Even though from here on out, I might just start calling you FG... Short for Fairy Godfather you know?"

He laughed. "Alright. See you later."

CHAPTER 6

The next morning, Carmen woke up with the dream she'd been having that night fresh on her mind. It was a crazy dream. Downright ridiculous. In her dream she'd had on a long beautiful gown — about like the one Cinderella had had on in the movie. And her new boss was in a tux driving her to some ball. They'd danced, then shared a sweet kiss.

She touched her lips with her finger. It all had felt so real.

"Your butt is definitely attracted to him," she whispered under her breath. "Now you going to bed dreaming about the man. What's gonna be next? You throwing yourself at him?"

She shook her head at that thought. Then she figured that it had been the seven years she'd gone without a man that was the problem. *Yeah, that's what it is. Now the first decent brotha who shows up in my face is staying on my mind because of all that. It's gonna pass soon enough.*

She got out of bed and started her day.

<<<<<>>>>>

"Morning, morning, sunshine. Thank you for the cheesecake that you left in the fridge for me last night. I woke up this morning and found it. Me and the Mr. had it for breakfast." Mrs. Ridley laughed. She winked her eye. "We added some fresh strawberries to it to make it healthy. We enjoyed it."

"Well, I'm certainly glad that you and Mr. Ridley liked it. The cheesecake was really for you. I wanted to do something special for you for how good you've been to me. Don't tell Mr. Ridley, but I'm buying him a special gift, too."

Mrs. Ridley laughed again. "I hope he's gonna be willing to share his gift with me."

Carmen shook her head. "I'm buying him an Atlanta Falcons mug. I'm sure you can sneak it from time to time and have your coffee in it."

Mrs. Ridley shook her head. "I'll pass on that one, baby doll." She pulled the loaf of bread she'd been baking out of the oven. "Now on a different subject, how did your date go last night with my nephew?"

A faraway look of remembrance came into Carmen's eyes. "It really wasn't a date, Mrs. Ridley. But I enjoyed myself. That nephew of yours is good company."

Mrs. Ridley could tell from the look on the girl's face standing in front of her that she had indeed enjoyed herself. And she could also tell that Carmen wasn't ready to admit to having a thing for Kevin. Mrs. Ridley smiled to herself. *I better leave that alone before I ruin things for my nephew and scare that poor girl away. He just might not forgive me if I do that.*

"Something sure do smell good in here. Is it you, Carmen?"

Carmen turned around and smiled at Janelle, who'd just stepped into the kitchen. "Morning, Janelle. It's the blueberry bread that Mrs. Ridley just baked. Imma let it cool down for about five minutes. Then I'm gonna beg her for a big slice. You know how Mrs. Ridley be throwing down in the kitchen. I'm sure gonna miss her food when my term is up and I have to move out of here."

Janelle took a seat at the kitchen table. "Oh, that's right. Your term's only for six months. Mine's a year... well really fifteen months. But I like it here, so I'm not counting. I guess you had a good time last night... huh?"

"Yeah. Like I was just telling Mrs. Ridley. It was a'ight."

"If you're up to having more fun, I have tickets to Six Flags. I know you don't have anything to do today, so you wanna hit 'em up with me?"

Carmen loved amusement parks. "Alright, Janelle. I'm up for that. I can even pay you for my ticket."

Janelle shook her head. "Nope. You ain't paying me

for nothing. I'm treating you. Be ready to roll at noon."

Five minutes later, Mrs. Ridley was once again alone in her kitchen. Janelle and Carmen had just walked out. *Janelle's a mess. I seen the way she been looking at Carmen. She been looking at her the way a hungry man looks at a three-course dinner. I hope she ain't about to try to turn that girl out.*

<<<<<>>>>>

Janelle and Carmen spent the entire day at Six Flags. A little past nine that night, Carmen followed Janelle through the front door of Halo House, toting the big teddy bear that Janelle had insisted that she let her win for her.

"You have a good time with me today, Carmen?"

"Yeah, girl. Six Flags was off the chain. I hadn't been up in there since I was sixteen. Mr. Pittman took my computer programming class back in high school. I was in the eleventh grade."

Janelle had to suppress her frown. *I done had a good day with her ass, and she had to bring up that joker.*

"You falling for Mr. Pittman or something, Carmen?"

"Naw, boo. He's just been helping me out. I appreciate him for that. The real question should be:

Are you going to church with me on Sunday? The other day, you said you might. Now I wanna know something for sure."

Janelle had thought about it, but she didn't have any real intentions of going to church with Carmen. She'd been tempted, but she didn't want to be criticized for being a lesbian by no church folk. Truth was, she was starting to fall for Carmen. However, now that Mrs. Ridley's nephew was in the picture, she'd do anything to have a little extra time with her. Therefore, she smiled and said, "Yeah. I'll roll up in the church with you on Sunday, Carmen."

Carmen cheesed. "For real, Janelle?"

"Yeah. For real, girl."

Carmen figured that her talks with Janelle about the Bible were starting to get in her head. *Well, amen, Lord. We're making progress*.

"I'll see you tomorrow," Carmen said.

"Yeah. Imma go to the kitchen and get me a glass of juice or something. See you tomorrow, Carmen." She winked her eye and laughed. "You pretty little thing you."

By now, Carmen was used to Janelle saying things like that. So, she didn't pay her friend's parting words too much attention.

When Janelle made it into the kitchen, Mrs. Ridley was in there already. "You and Carmen have yourselves a good time over at the Six Flags, Janelle?"

Janelle nodded her head. "Yes, ma'am. We sure did."

Not taking a break from her task of loading the dishwasher, Mrs. Ridley said, "I think Carmen has the hots for my nephew. And I believe he likes her, too. Bout time he found himself a nice, young lady to be interested in. He was married at one time — he's divorced now. His ex-wife was a real piece of work. Ended up on heroine and on the streets. My Kevin dang near lost everything he had behind that girl."

"So he deserted his wife when she really needed him?" Janelle's voice was full of sarcasm when she added, "That sounds like a real winner move right there."

"He didn't desert her. It was the other way around. Dominique was a real pretty girl. She looked just like a young Beyonce. Apparently some no-good drug dealer wanted her to marry him — in her messed up state and everything. She left my nephew and hooked up with her supplier."

Mrs. Ridley shook her head. "But that was a bad move on her part. Her new man got himself gunned down out there in them streets. Last I heard, Dominique's hanging out in trap houses on the south side. She out there tricking — or whatever else she gotta do — to get her next fix."

Janelle heard Mrs. Ridley out. When she'd finished speaking, Janelle took her glass of juice and left the kitchen. When she got back into her own room, she sat down on her bed. *I'm gonna have to figure out what I'm gonna do about all of this. I want Carmen. If you ask me, us being friends is just the next step to us being lovers. That girl is special.*

She set her glass of juice down on the nightstand and deserted it. She picked up her pack of Newport's, instead. She decided to head out to the porch and have herself a smoke. As she stood out there puffing on her cigarette, an idea began forming itself in her mind.

By the time she'd finished her Menthol 100, she had a smile on her face. *I know what I gotta do now.*

Three Days Later:

Carmen loved going to church. And what she loved even more this particular Sunday was the fact that her new friend, Janelle, had decided to go with her. Lisa had just made bail, and she'd agreed to go with Carmen, too. In fact, she was picking them up from Halo House.

When the pastor made the altar call, Janelle decided to make her way up to the front of the church. She wasn't interested in turning her life over to Christ. But she wanted to make a good impression on

Carmen. She kneeled there at the altar and allowed the pastor to pray over her. She even forced a couple of tears out of her eyes — she wanted to make everything look legit.

Sitting with Lisa in a pew with the rest of the congregation, Carmen had tears in her eyes as Janelle accepted Jesus into her life. Lisa, on the other hand, sat there frowning at everything. *This Janelle girl is trying to be slick. Her ass ain't interested in no Jesus. I wonder what her damn theatrical performance is all about. Somebody should hand her butt an Oscar...a Golden Globe or shit.*

Janelle had to go to work right after church services were over with, so Lisa dropped her off at The Auto Parts World. Then her and Carmen hit the road on their way to eat an early dinner. Lisa wasn't in the money like she'd used to be, so there would be no expensive dinner at Red Sizzler that particular day.

"You want some KFC, Carmen?"

Carmen nodded her head. "Yeah. I think I can go for some original recipe. And I'm paying since you were nice enough to drive us over to the church."

Lisa frowned. "Thanks, boo. I ain't in the money like I used to be. I'm gonna have to try to sale this car to put some duckies in my pocket. I figure I should be able to get at least thirty-five grand out of it... it's only a couple years old and it costed ninety-eight new. The Feds gonna have Big Ron locked up for a long time —

his crew, too — so he ain't gonna be able to kick me down with no cash. Shoot, I'm lucky they let my ass out on a misdemeanor."

"How did you manage that, Lisa? You take a plea or something?"

"Naw, no plea bargain. When the Po-Po busted up in the club, I pretended that I was just in there hanging out. I ain't say nothing to them about me working there running the tables. Plus, I think the officer who wrote me up down at the precinct liked me or something. You shoulda seen me up in there. I was pretending like I'd just been invited there by a friend...I told him I hadn't expected any illegal activities to be going on. I even cried girl — 'bout like your new lezzy friend Janelle did when she was up in the church today faking the funk."

Carmen shook her head. "I'm glad that you're not facing hard time, boo. But I don't think Janelle was playing."

A '*girl-please*' look came on Lisa's face. "She just trying to pull the wool over your eyes, Carmen. I don't know for what reason, but she is."

"I don't think so, Lisa. Janelle's trying to get her life back on track, about like what I'm doing. That's all."

Lisa kinda sensed that there wasn't going to be anything that she was going to be able to say to convince her girl of the truth of the situation — especially seeing that she didn't have any proof whatsoever. "I just hope she ain't trying to do you foul, Carmen. She gonna have hell to pay from these hands right here if she is."

It felt good to know that somebody had her back, but Carmen really didn't think Lisa had anything to worry about where Janelle was concerned. *Janelle's decent.*

Since neither one of them had felt like eating their food in the car, they decided to just go inside the restaurant. They'd almost finished eating when Mr. Pittman walked over to their table.

"Looks like great minds think alike. There's nothing like a little KFC after church. Based on your dress, I'm assuming that's where you ladies just came from."

"Hey, boss. Yep. We just got back from Sunday service. And thanks for the heads up on buying your uncle that Atlanta Falcons stuff. He loved it. And your auntie of course loved her cheesecake. She told me that me and you gonna have to go out to dinner together again... You know, since we brought them back gifts after the first time."

Wait a sec... her butt dating Mr. Pittman? That's what Lisa had just thought to herself. Then she gave Mr. Pittman a smile. "Good to see you again, Teach."

Kevin grinned at Lisa. "It's good to see you, too, Lisa. And it's even better to see that you decided to get your praise on today."

"Yeah."

"Well, I guess I'll go ahead and place my order before the line gets too long." He looked at Lisa. "Once again, it was good seeing you again, Lisa. And I'll see you tomorrow morning, Carmen."

After he'd walked away, Lisa said, "You two trying to hook up or something? That's why y'all went out to dinner...and why he said he'll see you in the morning?"

Carmen shook her head. "Naw, girl. Mr. Pittman ain't interested in my behind. I told you when you picked me up this morning that he gave me a job... Right?"

"Yeah. But what does that have to do with him taking you out to dinner?"

"He took me out to celebrate me finally being employed. That's all."

"I think he likes you, Carmen. I saw the way he was looking at you when the two of you were talking."

"You wrong about that, Lisa." She shook her head. "I don't know what's the problem with folks nowadays. Can't a male and a female go out to celebrate a thing without people thinking that the two of them trying to hook up?"

"So somebody else told you that they think he likes you, too? Is that what you're saying?"

Carmen sighed. "Not exactly. But a couple of people hinted at it. They weren't as vocal as you are about everything, though." Then she smiled. "But I wouldn't have expected anything less out of you, Lisa...seeing that you always tell it like it is. Your butt been like that ever since we were back in elementary school."

Lisa grinned as well. "You know I don't mince my words, boo." She sucked her teeth. "Shoot...ain't nobody got no bridle on my mouth. That's the for real truth right there."

Lisa's cell phone began ringing. She flipped over the device on the table and frowned. "That's my mama calling. I told you I had to move back in with her after Big Ron got himself locked up. I was supposed to have picked her up a half hour ago to take her grocery shopping. She probably gonna be talking some mess about kicking me out of her house now."

"You can go ahead and leave, Lisa. I know how your mama is, girl."

"You sure about that, Carmen? How you gonna get home?"

Carmen smiled. "Don't worry about me, boo. I still have two days worth of free bus passes on my card. I'll just take MARTA."

Lisa began to stand up from her seat. "You sure you alright with taking the bus, Carmen?"

"Girl, bye. I'm gonna be just fine. Your mama lives way on the opposite side of town. If you try to take me back to Halo House, you're not gonna make it home for another forty-five minutes...depending on traffic, maybe an hour."

"Alright, Carmen. Give your ol' bestie a hug till next time. It sure is nice hanging with you again, girl."

Exactly three minutes later, Carmen was sitting outside on a bench at the bus stop waiting for the number 120. She was glad that she'd only need one transfer to get her to her destination. She considered that to be a blessing. However, she couldn't help but look forward to the day she'd be able to actually afford a whip of her own again.

"Hey, Carmen. Need a ride back to Halo House?"

She'd been so absorbed in reading her Bible, that she hadn't noticed that Mr. Pittman had rolled up and parked a few feet away from the bus stop. Yeah, she'd heard his car. She just hadn't thought it was anyone looking for her, so she hadn't paid the BMW any attention.

She gave him a smile. "Taking me home isn't gonna mean that you're about to be going out of your way, is it? In other words...I'm not about to be a burden am I?"

He'd actually intended on going straight home to his own house. But he'd gladly take a detour if it meant that he'd get to spend some extra one on one time with Carmen. He shook his head. "Nope. You're not gonna be a burden at all." He got out of the car and went and opened the passenger-side door. "Come on, Cinderella. Your chariot awaits."

A girl who was sitting next to Carmen on the bench smiled and said out loud, "You can take me home if she don't wanna go, handsome. I don't live too far away from here."

Carmen stood up at that point. She flashed the girl a quick grin. "I'm going."

Later on that Night:

Carmen pulled back the covers on her bed and slid between her cool cotton sheets. As soon as her head hit the pillow, she began reflecting back over her entire day.

When her thoughts got to the part of the afternoon in which she'd run into Mr. Pittman, she smiled. Instead of going straight back to Halo House, he'd convinced her to make a quick detour to the park — all because she'd told him about how she used to like feeding the ducks there when she was a little girl.

He'd given her half of one of his biscuits and she'd fed God's little creatures.

Carmen had had a good time with the man out there in that park. He was so easy to talk to. For that reason, a whole three hours passed by without them even realizing it.

"Lord," she whispered under her breath. "It would be so easy to fall for a man like him. I never had a male in my life who treated me like he does."

She sighed and closed her eyes trying to get to sleep. She wasn't exactly sure how she felt about all of that.

CHAPTER 7

Carmen was ready and waiting for her ride bright and early the following morning. Needless to say, she was more than a little excited about her first day on her new job.

As Carmen settled herself into the passenger-side seat of her old teacher's vehicle, Janelle looked out one of the top floor windows of Halo House and frowned.

Janelle had heard all about Kevin bringing Carmen home yesterday and she didn't like it one little bit — just like she didn't like how he'd opened his truck door for her that morning and placed his hand under her elbow to help her into the vehicle.

She thought about the plan that she'd come up with to ensure that Carmen and Mr. Pittman never became a couple. "I'm not ready to act on it yet. So, in the meantime, I'm gonna have to treat Carmen extra nice...show her just how special she is."

Janelle smiled. "I think I'll get her some roses — the pink ones she said she liked. Just to brighten up her first day at her new job."

Jarrod tiptoed behind Janelle and peeped out the window, too. "What you looking at, girl?" When he saw Carmen riding away with Kevin Pittman, Jarrod laughed and began singing Whitney Houston's old song, *Heartbreak Hotel*.

He patted Janelle on the back. "Your heart just gone be broke over Carmen, Janelle. I keep telling you, she ain't down for kicking it with you like that. She want her a real man — someone 'bout like myself. Not a substitute like you."

Janelle narrowed her eyes at Jarrod and swiped his hand off her shoulder. "I done told your ass to stop touching me, fool. Keep it up...you gonna see which one of us is the real man. My money's on me, not you."

Jarrod grabbed his crotch. "Oh, okay. Let's drop our pants right out here and see." He shook his head. "I don't care how butch you leaning, you wasn't born with one of these."

Janelle felt like punching Jarrod in the face. But she knew if she did that, she'd get herself kicked out of Halo House. And she couldn't have that happening. It would jeopardize her parole and she'd be right back in lockup. *I don't want that.*

She shook her head and walked away. "I ain't got no time for fooling around with the likes of you, Jarrod," she threw back over her shoulder.

Doing fifteen years in a maximum security prison

had taken most of the feminine edge off of Janelle. As she walked away, she told herself that if she ever met Jarrod on the streets — after she'd been released from under parole — she was kicking his ass.

Across Town:

Carmen was a smart girl, so she was quickly learning the ropes at her new job. The day flew by in a flash. Before she knew it, four-thirty had arrived — which meant it was time for her to clock out and go home.

She walked out to the parking lot with Mr. Pittman and got into his truck.

Right after they took off, she glanced over at him and said, "You don't think people are gonna think it's weird that you're driving me to work and taking me home each day, do you, Mr. Pittman?"

He smiled. "Nope. Quite a few of the teachers and faculty members here carpool." He pointed over at an SUV that was leaving the parking lot ahead of them. "That's Mr. Andretti — one of our science teachers. The woman beside him is Mrs. Carson, she teaches English. And the woman in the back seat is Ms. Dawson — she's also a science teacher."

He widened his smile. "Carpooling… It's all about

101

saving the environment you know. Global warming and all. Every little bit helps."

Carmen was relieved to hear that. She'd just started her new job. She didn't need rumors being spread about her. She was hoping to make some new friends at her place of employment.

"Feel relieved?" he asked her.

She lifted her lips in a tiny smile. "Yeah. You know how people can be sometimes."

Because of her concerns, he knew right then and there that once the two of them started in a relationship, he was keeping things on the down-low for a little while. Meaning he intended on keeping their relationship to himself. He didn't want Carmen to feel uncomfortable.

He continued speaking. "I noticed that you brought a law book with you to school today, and that you were studying it during your lunchbreak..."

"Yeah." She smiled. "I'm not giving up on trying to pass the bar."

"I'm glad to hear that, Carmen. You got a ballpark date of when you're trying to take it?"

"I figure some time within the next two years. I need to save a couple thousand dollars for fees and such. That couple thousand isn't refundable if I don't pass it, so it needs to be extra money that I've saved. And I need to be off parole — I'll have a better shot at passing the character test part of it if I'm not on parole."

"Oh, okay. I understand."

They chatted about work for the rest of the ride back to Halo House. When Carmen walked through the front door of her temporary home, she ran into Mrs. Ridley, who was wearing a frown on her face. Mrs. Ridley was normally a very positive, upbeat type of person. So, Carmen immediately became concerned about what was wrong.

"What's done happened, Mrs. Ridley?"

Mrs. Ridley shook her head. "Nothing, baby. Janelle left a gift in the kitchen for you...before she left for work this afternoon."

Mrs. Ridley wasn't saying anything to Carmen, but it was the gift from Janelle that was causing the frown on her face.

Carmen walked into the kitchen and saw a vase of pink roses with a card attached to them. She smiled. Then she turned around and looked at Mrs.Ridley, who was following her. "Uh-oh. Sookie, sookie now. I see Mr. Ridley's getting his romance game on. Your flowers are beautiful, Mrs. Ridley."

Mrs. Ridley shook her head. "Them roses ain't for me, baby. It's the gift that I was telling you Janelle left in here for you."

Carmen walked over and took a look at the card. It read: *Hope you had a great day at work. Congrats on getting a job.*

Carmen thought it was sweet of Janelle to have sent her the flowers. She bent down and sniffed them. They even smelled sweet.

"Now I like Janelle well enough, Carmen — else she wouldn't be up in my halfway house. But you ain't about to switch teams and start messing around with her, are you?"

Carmen shook her head. She didn't say anything inappropriate to the woman, because she knew Mrs. Ridley was coming from a place of honest concern. "I'm straight, Mrs. Ridley. I already told Janelle that... Several times. She sent me the flowers because she's trying to be nice. That's all."

Mrs. Ridley was pushing sixty, so she'd seen a lot of things in her lifetime. She actually had a cousin who was close to her own age who was a lesbian. She'd seen her cousin, Nadine, turn quite a few straight women out.

Mrs. Ridley didn't have anything per se against people who were gay. She just felt like that type of lifestyle was against the way God wanted people living. And she had a soft, protective place in her heart for Carmen.

The middle-aged woman decided that she'd said all she had to say on that particular subject for now. Therefore, she grinned and said, "Okay, Carmen. Enough of all that... How did your first day on the job go?"

Now that was a subject that Carmen wanted to talk about. She took a seat at the kitchen table and began filling Mrs. Ridley in on the details of her day.

The next four days of the work week blew by in a flash. Before Carmen knew it, Saturday had arrived — and with it the date that she and Mr. Pittman were going to have at the Midtown Gospel Fest.

Just like the previous weekend when he'd taken her out to dinner to celebrate having a job, she took extra care with getting herself dressed.

She refused to lie to herself about things anymore. She'd spent all week working for the man, and the high school crush that she'd had on Mr. Pittman had morphed into a grown-tail woman type of crush.

She had to literally keep herself reading her Bible several times a day to keep lustful thoughts about him from entering her mind.

Her attraction to her boss went well beyond the physical. She was drawn to his mind, too. She was drawn to his heart. She liked how positive he was, how kind and considerate.

Like most young women her age, Carmen secretly dreamed of having a good man in her life. Not just in her life — but as a husband. She knew for a fact that if Mr. Pittman ever decided to step to her in a man/woman relationship type of way, she was going to be all for getting to know him better. She was going to be more than willing to see whether a relationship between the two of them would work out.

As she finished beating up her face, she frowned at her reflection in her mirror. "But he ain't gonna be interested in you like that," she whispered to her mirror image. "He's probably looking for a woman who got her ish together." She let out a sarcastic little bark of laughter. "Your butt just got outta prison, and you living in a halfway house," she derided under her breath.

Then the little voice in her head reasoned: *But he started from the bottom, too. He told you about how he grew up. He wasn't born with no silver spoon in his mouth. He understands the concept of the come-up.*

The clean version of Drake's old song, *Started from the Bottom*, popped up in her head. She smiled.

"Maybe we *would* have a chance if he was interested in me like that," she finally said.

Ten minutes later, Kevin was wowed by the vision of loveliness that stood in front of him when Halo House's door opened.

"You look beautiful, Carmen."

106

She smiled. "Thank you, Mr. Pittman. I'm ready to go if you are."

He escorted her out to his BMW and they started on their way. During the week, they'd decided that in addition to the Gospel Fest, they were also going to do dinner together that particular day. Since Carmen had always wanted to try Thai food, they stopped by a restaurant called, Thai Kitchen and Bar that was located in Peachtree Hills. The Gospel Fest that day lasted almost five hours, and Carmen enjoyed every second of it. Quite a few of her favorite international Gospel performers took the stage.

As they sped back towards Halo House, Kevin glanced over at his date for the evening and smiled. "You're good company, Carmen. You sure know how to have a Holy Ghost good time."

She laughed at that. "You, too. People have to understand that just because a person's trying to follow Christ, it don't mean they don't know how to party — now I'm talking in a righteous type of way, of course."

"Yeah. I like your view on that, Carmen." He began thinking about his ex-wife, Dominique. Dominique and Carmen were polar opposites. His ex-wife hadn't wanted anything to do with God. In fact, many times, it seemed as if Dominique had wanted to run as far away from God as she could.

Kevin had been young when he'd fallen for

Dominique. All he'd seen was how beautiful she was on the outside. He hadn't been smart enough back then to realize that his prospective wife's relationship with the Creator was just as important as her relationship with him. *Even more important*, he thought to himself. *If me and Carmen make it that far, I know I won't be having that type of problem with her. God is her everything.*

"What is it, Mr. Pittman?" She could tell that something heavy was on his mind.

He lifted his lips in a tiny smile again. "Nothing's wrong, Carmen." He reached across the console and took her hand into his. He gave it a little squeeze. "Everything's perfectly fine."

Them holding hands like that felt so right to Carmen. When he removed his hand from hers a few seconds later and placed it back on the steering wheel, she felt like all the warmth had left her fingers. She'd enjoyed his touch.

When they made it back to Halo House, Kevin cut the engine to his ride and glanced over at Carmen. He smiled. "Well, Cinderella...I guess your coach is about to turn back into a pumpkin and you'll be back in the truck again tomorrow."

"Oh, your truck is practically new, Mr. Pittman. It has a leather interior with what looks like all the upgrades. I hardly think your F-350 — with its nice chrome rims and all — is a pumpkin." She laughed.

"Far from it. But I know what you mean if that makes any difference...no cruising tomorrow in the Beemer."

He smiled again. "Yeah. That's what I mean." He pressed the button to unlock the doors. "I'm about to go around and get your door for you so I can walk you up to the house." He winked his eye real quick. "We can't have you missing curfew, now can we? My Aunt Michelle might just take a switch to me if that happened. She would know for sure that it was all my fault. That I was enjoying your company so much that I didn't want to let you go."

Carmen doubted if his auntie would take a switch to him. But she didn't want to miss her curfew all the same. She had too much respect for the Ridleys to pull a stunt like that.

She allowed him to walk her to the door. Just like a week ago, when they'd gone out to dinner together, it felt a little awkward when they finally made it to the front porch.

"Well, I guess I'll see you tomorrow, Mr. Pittman."

"Yeah. See you tomorrow, Carmen." He suddenly reached his hand into his suit pocket and handed her something wrapped in tissue paper. "We were having such a good time at the Gospel Fest that I almost forgot about this."

With a curious expression on her face, she took the item that he'd handed her. "Um...what is this?"

"Unwrap it when you get inside. You'll see what it

is. I think you're gonna like it."

She nodded her head. "Alright, boss. Thank you. I'll see you bright and early tomorrow morning. Okay?"

"Alright."

A few minutes later, Carmen was standing in her bedroom. She hadn't turned on the lights yet, but it was a full moon that night, which meant she could see plenty good in her room at that moment. She walked over to her window and began unwrapping her gift. She'd only pulled back the paper partially when the item that had been hidden up until now caught the moonlight and threw off a little glint.

She suspected it was some type of metal. A few more peels to the paper revealed the sterling silver and diamond crucifix necklace that she'd been admiring at one of the vending stalls at the event. The piece of jewelry had been on sale for a hundred and sixty dollars. Carmen now had a job, but that was still a little too rich for her blood.

"He didn't," she whispered under her breath. However, the piece of jewelry in her hand proved that he indeed had.

Then she read the little notecard that he'd included with it. In his own handwriting, it read: *Please don't turn this gift down, Carmen. It's not like I can take it back. The vendors aren't going to be there tomorrow. ENJOY IT CINDERELLA. The ball's not over yet.* He'd closed out the note with a smiley face that made her smile, too.

Carmen sat down on her bed with her gift in her hand. She sighed to herself.

"Lord, this man is something else. It's gonna be so danggone easy for my butt to fall for him. I can't believe a guy like him isn't taken. As far as brothas go, he's a certified catch. He loves the Lord, he's handsome, can pay all his bills — and probably all of mine, too. And that big ol' juicy heart of his..." She nodded her head. "Oh yeah... He a catch alright."

When she heard a light knock at her bedroom door, she got up to see who was there. She suspected it was Janelle. Turned out her suspicion was correct.

Janelle grinned. "Hey, sweet thang. I just wanted to tell you goodnight."

Carmen smiled in return. "Goodnight yourself, Janelle. And once again, thanks for the roses. They brightened up my day."

Janelle laughed. "That's what I was shooting for, boo." She noticed the piece of jewelry in Carmen's hand. She pointed at it. "That's nice. Real pretty."

"Yeah. It was a gift from a friend."

Janelle had to suppress her frown. The piece of jewelry looked expensive. She suspected that it was from her competition for Carmen's affections. "Hmmm...was it Lisa who gave it to you?"

Carmen shook her head. "Naw. It was actually Mr. Pittman. We went to the Gospel Fest and they had vendors there selling stuff. Girl, I didn't even know he'd bought it. We walked past the booth and I'd told him how much I liked it. He walked me to the front door of Halo House a few minutes ago. Handed me something wrapped in tissue and told me not to open it until I got inside." She smiled again. "This is what I found when I peeled back the wrapping paper."

Janelle nodded her head. "That's nice, Carmen. Look, Imma gone 'head to bed. I'm sure you gotta get up early tomorrow morning for work."

"Yeah. I do. A sista got to make that paper. I gotta get them dollars."

"I hear you, boo. Night, Carmen."

"Night, Janelle."

When Janelle got back to her own room, she wanted to punch a hole in the wall. But since she suspected the noise and the damage from doing that would get her kicked out of Halo House, she punched her bed instead. "That nigga ain't 'bout to roll up in here and steal what's supposed to be mines!" she hissed under her breath. "I'm glad my ass is kicking my master plan into gear tomorrow!"

CHAPTER 8

Janelle left Halo House bright and early the following morning. It had taken a whole lot of asking around to finally find the person she was looking for. But two days ago, she'd found out what places and whatnot the person frequented.

Janelle knew for a fact that where she was going could get her parole overturned if she got caught there. Therefore, before she knocked on the door of the trap house off of Madison, she looked carefully around her scanning for five-o.

"Who you looking for?" A gruff-sounding voice asked.

Janelle had scoped out the password to get her through the front door so she responded with, "Johnny thirty-seven."

The door of the place was opened for her and the stench of weed, mustiness, smoke, and Lord knows what else assaulted her nostrils.

Since she knew she had to play like she was a druggie, she began scratching herself and acting a little jumpy.

113

"Where Dominique at? She supposed to have a hit she sharing with me."

The man pointed over in the corner at a girl who would've been a Beyoncé look-alike — that is if she wasn't all drugged out.

Janelle knew right away that it was going to be a struggle getting this Dominique girl somewhat clean. But seeing that she was Kevin's ex-wife — who Janelle had heard from Mrs. Ridley herself that he used to be in love with — she figured that getting Dominique clean was exactly what she had to do.

I'm real persuasive, Janelle thought to herself. *I've talked people into doing worse things before. I can convince this druggie to go to rehab. In twenty-one days, she gonna be looking decent enough. Then I'm gonna get her up into Halo House and all in Kevin Pittman's face. Carmen cute and all. But when he sees his angel here all cleaned up, he gonna want her back. All I have to do is whisper in Dominique's ear — remind her how great things used to be when her and her husband were together. Then that's gonna be all she wrote. Dominique is gonna go after her man, leaving me a straight path to Carmen's broken little heart. I can already tell that Carmen's already falling in love with that fool.*

114

Across Town at Halo House:

Kevin pulled out of the driveway of his aunt's halfway house. Then he glanced over at Carmen and smiled. "I'm glad you decided to keep my gift. It looks good on you."

From the look of honest admiration in the man's eyes, Carmen blushed. She lightly placed her fingers on the sterling silver cross. "Thank you for buying it for me, Mr. Pittman. I don't know why you bought it...but thanks. I love it."

"I bought it because when you laid your eyes on it, your face lit up. I wanted to see that glow on your pretty face again...just like now."

She wanted to ask him why her happiness mattered to him, but for some reason, she decided not to. She decided to just let things be as they were.

Kevin's day with Carmen was moving along just fine. That is until one of the science teachers decided to show up in his office.

"Hey, Antoine. What brings you up here to the front end this time of day? What can I do for you?"

Mr. Cherry shook his head at what Kevin had just asked, but his eyes were all on Carmen. Not looking away from her, he smiled. "Oh, I don't need anything from you today, Principal Pittman. I'm here to talk to Ms. Flood."

Carmen grinned at the man. "Me? What can I do

for you this afternoon? Technically, it's still morning since it's eleven forty-three. But you know what I mean."

"I was hoping that I could convince you to go out to lunch with me today. That new sandwich shop not too far from here."

Carmen had been wanting to give them a try. Seeing that she didn't have a car — and the bus wouldn't have gotten her there and back to school during her lunch hour — she hadn't been as of yet. She liked Antoine Cherry. He seemed like one of the good guys — and he'd told her he was saved.

She gave him a smile. "Okay. I break at noon. Is that good?"

Antoine had already looked into all of that. In other words, he knew exactly what time Carmen's lunch period started. He'd asked another one of the vice principals on staff for the info.

At exactly noon, as Antoine Cherry opened the office door and walked Carmen out, Kevin frowned. He knew that the man was really feeling Carmen. He could tell from the look in his eyes.

The realization suddenly hit Kevin that he had competition. *My Aunt Michelle was right. I'm trying to take things slow — almost a snail's pace. But if I move too slow, I might lose her.*

Kevin knew that his Mack game was tight whenever he needed it to be. *He nodded his head. I'm*

116

about to eliminate the competition. Sorry Antoine, but not sorry.

Since he was a man of faith, he said a quick prayer that God would have his back in whatever moves he was about to make to secure his position in Carmen's heart. *I'm falling in love, Lord. I can't lose her before we even get started.*

Carmen had a good time eating lunch with Antoine Cherry. He had a pleasant personality and a good sense of humor, which may her feel really comfortable around him. She kind of suspected that he liked her, but she wasn't exactly sure about that. He was good looking. He was nice and all. But he didn't hold a candle to Kevin Pittman — not in Carmen's eyes.

<<<<<>>>>>

At twelve fifty-nine, Carmen walked back into Kevin's office. Still thinking about a joke that Antoine had told her, she had a big ol' Kool-Aid grin on her face.

Kevin tried his best not to be jealous, but he couldn't stop himself. He knew feelings like jealousy were straight from the devil, so he fought to stomp the wayward emotion under his feet.

He forced himself to put a tiny smile on his handsome face. "You have a good time at lunch,

Carmen?"

"Yeah. The food was good. So was the company. So I have to admit, I had a good time."

He nodded his head. "That's good. You ready to get back to work?"

"Yeah. Of course. That's what you guys pay me for — work."

Carmen took her seat behind her desk. She could tell something was a little off with her boss — despite the fact that he tried to cover it up with a smile. She just didn't know what that something was.

She didn't want bad air between them, so she decided to try to do a little investigating. "You had me handling your emails this morning, Mr. Pittman. Did I misfile some of them or something?"

"No. Your work on the emails was flawless, Carmen."

"Well, did I not put the correct postage meter stamp on those letters from yesterday? Did some of them come back?"

"Nope, nothing came back."

Carmen would've asked him some more questions, but the office phone on her desk began ringing. She was forced to handle that call, and that was the end of her little line of inquiries.

The end of the workday couldn't get there quick enough for Carmen. She intended to talk to Mr. Pittman about what she'd obviously done wrong on the ride back to Halo House.

As soon as the truck pulled out of Pondfield Academy's parking lot, Carmen turned around in her seat and said, "Okay...I can tell that there's some type of tension between us. Can you please tell me what I did wrong so I can work on fixing it."

He sighed. Then, without looking over at her, he pulled the truck into a Target parking lot. He aimed for a secluded spot way in the back so that they could have some privacy.

Good, he's stopping so we can talk. We're getting somewhere.

Kevin turned around in his seat. His eyes met Carmen's. "I'm not the type of brotha who believes in side stepping around important issues." He took her hand into his. "Truth be told, I was jealous. That's what the problem was today, Carmen. Antoine Cherry stepped into that office and swooped you off to lunch. And I didn't like it."

Wait a second. He was jealous? He gotta have feelings for me if that's the case. Right?

He nodded his head. "Yeah. I'm really feeling you, Carmen. I'm falling for you, girl. I've been making little notes about everything about you...it ain't nothing that I don't like." He smiled. "Except maybe the fact that you snore. But I think that's a little cute, though."

She'd taken a nap at her desk during her lunch break one day during the previous week. That's how he knew she snored.

He placed his hand on the side of her cheek. "Well, what do you say? You gonna give me a chance? I mean *us* a chance?"

"I wasn't expecting any of this, Mr. Pittman. You're technically my boss. How is that gonna look at Pondfield? You and me dating?"

He was glad that she wasn't turning him down outright. Her question showed him that she was probably interested — *she just doesn't want to get caught up in any workplace drama. I can put a ton of respect on that.*

He smiled again. "Well, we can interact with each other the way we've been doing all along at work. Like you can keep calling me Mr. Pittman and I'll call you Ms. Flood. But on our private time, we're Kevin and Carmen. Will that work for you, sweetheart?"

Oh, Lord. He called me sweetheart. He's for real.

"What do you say, Carmen? Will you give us a chance? I can't get you out of my mind and I don't want to even try to."

She finally smiled at him. Then she nodded her head, prompting Kevin to dip his toward hers and place a soft kiss right on the corner of her lips.

"Thank you, Carmen. I just feel like I won the lottery. No telling how I'm gonna feel if you ever say you'd be willing to marry me." He was happy with the outcome of everything, so he chuckled at that. He felt like he'd just been graced with a big ol' blessing.

"Oh, I think you'll handle it just fine, Mr. Pittman...I mean *Kevin*."

He liked the way his name sounded rolling off of her luscious-looking lips. He liked it a whole lot. "Wanna go out right now to celebrate us officially dating? You know, instead of going straight over to Halo House?"

Carmen smiled. "Yeah. Let's do that."

<<<<<>>>>>

Two Hours Later:

Holding hands, Kevin walked Carmen up to the front door of Halo House. Then he did something that he'd been wanting to do almost since the day he'd first laid eyes on her again two months ago. He dipped his head and kissed her goodnight. Right on her luscious, plump lips.

That was their very first official kiss — excluding the off-center peck that he'd given her when he'd first asked if she'd start dating him earlier that evening. And it felt so good to Carmen being in her new boyfriend's arms. It felt so right.

Kevin was feeling the exact same way as Carmen. He'd kissed plenty of girls in his past — and he'd loved his ex-wife, Dominique. But being there with Carmen made him feel like he was drowning in a sea of pleasure — and he didn't want any type of escape from the mind-blowing, toe-curling, sensual abyss.

He'd never felt that way with any other woman. So he knew right then and there that Carmen was the girl for him. She was the sista that he wanted to spend the rest of his life with. He had no doubt at all in his mind of that fact.

As Kevin slowly pulled away from heaven, thus breaking their embrace, Carmen took several deep breaths to get herself back together. "Wow," she finally whispered as she slowly pulled her thumb over her kiss-swollen lips.

He smiled and gently caressed her cheek with his palm. "Yeah...that was something else wasn't it?"

She couldn't help but nod her head.

Still grinning he said, "See you bright and early tomorrow morning, Cinderella. After that kiss you just laid on me, I feel like a prince...not a frog anymore."

She laughed. "I think you got the wrong fairy tale, Bae. That wasn't Cinderella. That one was the Princess and the Frog. I think somebody's gonna need to brush up on their Disney movies."

He smiled. "Sure, babe. Until tomorrow, princess."

As he drove himself home, he couldn't help but think about the kids he wanted to someday have with Carmen. He was pretty much sure that they were gonna be into Disney — *especially our little girls*. He chuckled to himself. *I'm gonna have to at least have the stories straight.*

He knew that Carmen was his soulmate and he felt so blessed to finally have her in his once lonely life.

<<<<<>>>>>

Back at Halo House:

"Now I wasn't eavesdropping or being nosy, but I saw you and Kevin out there on the front porch smooching a minute ago, Carmen." Mrs. Ridley grinned. "I'm suspecting the two of you are a couple now. Am I right?"

Carmen had still been smiling because she felt good that she was now officially dating the man she'd slowly been falling for. But that smile turned into a frown upon hearing Mrs. Ridley's question. "Um, yeah...we're dating. I know I'm probably not the type of girl you envisioned with your nephew, but..."

Mrs. Ridley chuckled. Then she gave Carmen a warm hug. "Little girl...please. You're exactly the type of girl I want for my Knee Knee. Ain't you been listening to anything I been telling you about yourself, Carmen? You're a fine young lady. Saved, beautiful, courteous, nice to people...my nephew is blessed to have you in his life. That mess with you being locked up is just a hiccup. You done moved past that now."

123

She placed both of her hands on Carmen's arms. "God's got some mighty fine plans for you, Carmen. Mark my words on that. You hear?"

Carmen finally smiled again. "Okay, Mrs. Ridley. I guess I'd better go put on some work clothes so I can get to helping you around the house a little. Alright?"

Mrs. Ridley nodded her head. "Alright, sugar."

While Carmen was upstairs changing, Janelle made it back to Halo House from work. Mrs. Ridley knew how Janelle felt about Carmen. She of course didn't approve of it, so it gave her much pleasure to drop the news on Janelle about Kevin and Carmen dating.

"What did you say, old lady?"

"Old lady?" Mrs. Ridley began wagging her finger. "Now I done told your little behind not to keep calling me that, Janelle. Show some respect."

Janelle pulled her eyebrows together in a frown. "I'm sorry, Mrs. Ridley. What you just said shocked me. That's all."

Mrs. Ridley appreciated the apology, so she nodded her head and replied, "Okay. I suppose I can understand that. The fact that my Kevin and Carmen are dating was a surprise to me, too. I ain't gonna lie...I knew it was coming. But I thought it was gonna be a little later on than now." Then she laughed. "I really shouldn't be surprised, though. The men in my family are known for going after what they really want."

124

Janelle nodded her head. "Yeah, I'm sure they are, Mrs. Ridley." Her frown deepened. "I'm about to go up to my room now."

Mrs. Ridley waited until Janelle had disappeared upstairs before whispering under her breath, "Lord, I sure hope that puts an end to Janelle pining after Carmen. I hope she done figured out that she ain't gonna be able to lure that child over to the sinning side."

Mrs. Ridley knew that the spirit of Satan was real strong. So, she made it up in her mind that she was going to keep Carmen and Kevin as a couple on her daily prayer list. She shook her head. *Lord knows my nephew deserves to find him a good woman after all that mess he went through with his first wife.*

<<<<<>>>>>

The next four weeks passed by in a blur for Carmen. She knew she'd been attracted to Kevin in a big way, but now that they really were dating, she knew that attraction had morphed into her actually being in love.

Lisa smiled as she drove her and Carmen out of the driveway of Halo House. "Now that you got a bae, I hardly ever see your butt, Carmen Flood. So thanks for taking the time out of your day to hang with me this evening, girl."

Carmen couldn't disagree with anything that her

bestie was saying, because she knew it was all the truth. Carmen was spending the majority of her free time with Kevin.

Lisa had made some positive changes in her life and was now going to church every Sunday, so Carmen generally saw her on that day. But other than that, no — Carmen would be with her man, instead.

Lisa laughed. She reached over and patted Carmen's hand. "You don't have to apologize, boo. I know your butt's in love. If I had a good man like Kevin Pittman, I'd be all up in his face as much as possible, too." She signaled to change lanes then asked, "Why don't the two of you just go ahead and get married?" She smiled. "I *would* say just start shacking up together, but I know both of y'all take being saved real serious. Ain't gonna be none of that... Huh?"

Carmen shook her head. "Naw. Ain't gonna be none of that, Lisa." But she wasn't averse to the idea of marrying Kevin. *He's the man of my dreams. I love him so much. God done blessed me. He put my soulmate in my life, and I'm grateful for that.*

Across town, Kevin was feeling the exact same way. He and Carmen normally spent all of Saturday together. But this particular Saturday, she'd skipped out on him to have some quality time with her bestie.

He missed his bae something fierce.

"I wouldn't be feeling like that if her fine butt was coming home to me, to my bed," he whispered under his breath. "I wouldn't be missing her if she was sleeping in my arms every night."

Kevin's uncle, Nathan, had decided to watch the game with Kevin in his crib that day. Nathan placed his can of Coke on the coffee table. "What's wrong, Kev? And don't say nothing. I been seeing that look on your face off and on ever since you were a little boy."

Kevin rubbed a hand over the top of his head and frowned. His uncle was closer to him than his own father. The man had practically raised him. Therefore, he felt comfortable spilling his guts to him. "It's Carmen. I guess I'm missing her. That's all. We normally spend our Saturdays together. She dumped me today to hang with her friend, Lisa."

Nathan smiled. Then he chuckled. "When a man starts feeling like that, it generally means that he's about ready to get married."

It suddenly hit him. *Unc's right. I'm gonna ask her to marry me. That's what I'm about to do. Imma do it tomorrow after church.*

He grinned even harder because he knew his woman was going to say 'yes'. He could feel it all in his bones.

<<<<<>>>>>

Over at Halo House, Janelle laid down on her back on her bed. She pulled out the picture that she and Carmen had taken together at a photo booth the day they'd gone to Six Flags. She reached out and gently traced Carmen's pretty face on the photograph.

"Damn, you so sexy Carmen, and your fine ass don't even be trying to be."

Janelle felt like touching herself in her feminine areas, thus relieving some of the sexual tension that was building up in her just from looking at the picture of Carmen. After all, it wouldn't be the first time she'd done that with that very same snapshot.

"You gonna be mine, Carmen. You might be running around with that fool Kevin right now, but all of that is about to change."

A devious little smile planted itself on Janelle's face. Then she proceeded to go ahead and get her rocks off.

When she'd finished her business, she laid the picture of her and Carmen on her pillow. *Before long, I'm gonna have the real thing up in my room. Not no damn substitute.*

CHAPTER 9

Carmen woke up early the following morning, earlier than she usually did on Sundays. She'd set her alarm clock for eight like normal, but her body had awakened her at seven-thirty. Something in her spirit was telling her that there was going to be something special about this particular Sabbath day. She didn't know what her God had in store for her, but she knew it was something good.

She laid there in her bed reflecting on just how wonderful God was. "I can't imagine living my life without you, Lord. Thank you for everything you've done for me. And thank you for the moves you've been making in my girl Lisa's life, too. I've been praying and praying for her, and she's finally making her way over to you."

Carmen hadn't wanted to let go of her lifelong bestie. But she knew it was very possible that that would've eventually happened if Lisa had decided to keep going down the path that she'd been traveling on. *Our split wouldn't have been anything intentional. It would've happened gradually.*

129

Carmen already knew that Lisa would've naturally shied away from the God spirit that she intended on letting shine for the rest of her life.

Her mind then landed on Janelle. She'd been praying for Janelle, too. At first, Carmen had thought that Janelle was starting to open up her heart to Christ. Carmen frowned. Now she wasn't so sure about all of that.

She liked Janelle a whole lot. But Carmen was smart enough to realize that a body had to like and/or love some people from a distance. She knew that Janelle had the potential to become one of her lifelong friends. However, there was something a little off in their relationship.

Carmen shook her head. *I'm not exactly sure what that something is, Lord. But I'd sure appreciate it if you would fix it.*

Later on that Afternoon:

Church services had been lit that particular Sunday at Calvary Christian Center. Carmen always enjoyed herself at her house of worship, but her pastor obviously preached a message that touched a lot of people's hearts that particular day.

By the time everything was said and done, Carmen

figured that she shouldn't have even worn any make up. Her mascara had run, and so had her foundation. She'd cried her heart out to her God and worshipped with a vengeance that day.

The fact that her bestie had decided to finally respond to the altar call and commit herself to Christ had been the best part of the service for Carmen. She'd been praying for Lisa, and she was happy that the powerful God that she served had answered her prayers.

Kevin had gotten into the habit of attending Carmen's church more often than he attended his own. So he was there in the congregation, too.

After the pastor gave the closing remarks, Kevin escorted both Carmen and Lisa out of the sanctuary. Carmen gave her girl one last hug, then she and Kevin took off together in his BMW.

Carmen smiled over at her man. "I know I must look a mess, Bae."

Kevin shook his head. "You know you're always beautiful to me, right?"

Carmen began thinking about something that Mrs. Ridley had told her two weeks ago. The woman had said: *"True love will make a man overlook some of everything about his woman's appearance. Now I ain't saying a girl ought to let herself go. But what I just told you is the God's honest truth."*

Carmen then began thinking about the lyrics to one

of her favorite R&B classics — Don't Change by Musiq Soulchild. *I'll love you when your hair turns gray, I'll still want you if you gained a little weight. The way I feel for you will always be the same, just as long as your love don't change.*

Carmen glanced over at her man. *He must feel that way about me.*

All the same, she decided to pull out her compact and fix her face. All of that only took her a few minutes. When she glanced up, she realized that they weren't heading towards the restaurant that they'd agreed on having dinner at earlier in the week.

A look of confusion came into Carmen's eyes. "Bae, Abu's Moroccan Grille isn't downtown."

Kevin reached over and took her hand into his. He smiled. "I know. I wanted to take you somewhere else first. Then we'll go eat. It's a surprise. You okay with that?"

Carmen loved surprises, so of course she was alright with that.

Kevin laughed. "Look at my Cinderella over there with her eyes sparkling with excitement. I think I'm gonna have to surprise you more often... Just so I can see that look on your gorgeous face."

Carmen laughed, too. "When I woke up this morning, I knew this day was gonna be extra special — in a good kind of way." She leaned across the console and whispered in his ear, "You can always just tell me what my surprise is."

He shook his head. "Nope. I ain't saying a word. That would ruin your surprise. Now put your fine self back into your own seat, woman."

Kevin's sexual attraction to his lady was off the chain. He'd had to keep himself prayed up just to keep his hands off of her. He didn't think he'd prayed so much in his whole life, and he'd been saved going on eight years.

Carmen was familiar with the look in her man's eye. She'd had the same expression in her own where he was concerned — more than a time or two. *I think I'd better take his advice and keep myself over here in my own seat. No need flirting with temptation*. She wanted to wave her hand in front of her face because she suddenly felt hot — and not from the temperature in the BMW. *The temptation might just be too much for both of us to handle*.

She finally smiled. "Alright, Bae. I can be patient. You just watch me."

Fifteen minutes later, Kevin claimed a spot in a parking lot downtown. He came around and got Carmen's door. "We're almost there."

Carmen shrugged her shoulders. She had no idea where they were going or what this was all about. There were all types of trendy shops and restaurants in that part of town. They could've been going to any one of them. "Okay. Lead the way, sweetheart."

133

They walked for less than a minute, then Kevin opened the door of a jewelry store and walked Carmen inside. Right above one of the jewelry counters, there was a banner that read: *Carmen Flood, Will You Marry Me, Princess?* She realized the second she saw that thing that she'd wasted her time reapplying her makeup. Tears of joy were in her eyes all over again.

Kevin grinned. "Well sweetheart… Will you? I brought you here so that we could knock out two birds with one stone. You know, get engaged and get a ring for that pretty little finger of yours at the same time."

She was speechless…but only for a little while. Then she shouted, "Yes!"

The jewelry store attendant was smiling at the couple from behind the display counter. "I guess you'll be buying an engagement ring for sure today, Mr. Pittman."

You darn skippy, Carmen thought to herself.

Their after-church dinner that evening actually ended up being their personal engagement dinner. Instead of the borderline casual restaurant that Kevin had told Carmen he was taking her to, he'd taken her to an upscale place downtown. He'd made

134

reservations and everything. Carmen did indeed feel like a fairytale princess when they'd finished their day.

When he brought his car to a stop in Halo House's driveway that evening, it was close to seven. Since summer was quickly approaching, the days were longer. Therefore, there was still plenty of sunlight outside, and Carmen kept smiling as her platinum engagement ring with the 1.20 carat diamond glittered in the sunshine.

"If it's okay with you, sweetheart, I want to go ahead and make the announcement to Unc and Aunt Michelle."

Carmen nodded her head. "Yep. That's perfectly fine by me. I don't think your aunt and uncle are gonna be surprised, though."

Kevin grinned. He didn't think they were gonna be surprised either. It was no secret that he was in love with Carmen and wanted to marry her. Not to anyone. "Come on, sweetheart. Let's go let everyone know."

They had matching smiles on their faces when they walked into the foyer of Halo House that evening. However, Kevin's dropped as soon as they stepped foot into the kitchen.

"Hello, Kevin. You looking fine as eva, Bae. Long time no see." Dominique smiled and wrapped her arms around her ex-husband in a warm hug. She pretty much knew who Carmen was — Janelle had given her the 4-1-1 on the first day they'd met in that grungy trap house. But she didn't care. In her estimation, Carmen wouldn't be Kevin's boo-thang for much longer. "What? You ain't gonna give your wifey a hug in return?"

Kevin's frown deepened. "We're not married anymore, Dominique. I have the papers to prove it."

She laughed. "We always gonna be connected, Kevin. We were each other's first — first everything and I know you know what I'm talking about. People don't forget their firsts. And they never really fall out of love with them."

Kevin extracted himself out of her arms. He didn't respond to any of that. "What are you doing here, Dominique?"

"I just got outta rehab. I'm all clean now. A condition of the program I was in was that I had to have somewhere reliable to live once they sprung me. I was able to talk your Aunt Michelle into giving me a room."

As if on cue, Kevin's auntie walked into the kitchen and frowned. She hadn't wanted to let Dominique stay there at Halo House, but she hadn't had a choice. Dominique was privy to a secret that could rock Michelle's whole family. The Beyonce-lookalike standing in front of her had promised to keep her mouth shut if Michelle opened her home up to her. So that's what Michelle had done.

Kevin looked over at his aunt for confirmation.

Michelle couldn't completely banish the look of displeasure from her face. She nodded her head and said, "It's true. She's living here for the next six months."

Kevin refused to allow Dominique to ruin his and Carmen's special moment. He placed his arm protectively around Carmen's waist, smiled, and said, "Me and Carmen just got ourselves engaged." He lovingly looked his new fiancé in the eye and continued speaking. "Show my auntie the ring, Bae."

Carmen lifted her lips in a tiny grin and flashed her ring for Mrs. Ridley. This wasn't exactly how she'd envisioned their big reveal playing out, but Lord knows she intended to make the very best that she could of it.

Later on that Evening:

Carmen had been working long enough that she now could afford a cellphone. So sitting in her bedroom, she pulled out her phone and dialed her bestie's number. "Hey, Lisa...you not gonna believe what's happened."

"What, Carmen? From the sound of your voice, it seems like it's something good. You get a promotion or something at work?" She quickly added, "Wait a minute, it's a Sunday. You didn't go to work today. Shoot, the school ain't even open. Go ahead, tell me what I'm not gonna believe, boo."

"I'm getting married! Kevin popped the question this afternoon. It was so romantic. He took me downtown to Scheibler's. He had a banner over the jewelry counter that said: Carmen Flood, Will You Marry Me, Princess?" Just thinking about it, Carmen smiled. "I said yes and picked out my ring right there on the spot!"

Lisa was happy for her girl. She knew how much she loved Kevin. She grinned into her phone and said, "Congratulations, honey. But it's really not a surprise to me. I knew he was about to pop the question — Kevin ain't the type to believe in shacking up like most of them fools we used to kick it with. It was only a matter of time. Everybody could see how much in love the two of you were and are. Y'all gonna be together forever, boo."

That last part got Carmen to thinking about what had gone down when they'd stepped into the kitchen earlier that afternoon. "Yeah," she said under her breath. "Together forever."

"Uh-oh. I been knowing your butt long enough to know something ain't quite right. What is it, Carmen?"

Carmen shared all the details of what had happened with Dominique, Kevin's ex-wife.

"Hold on, wait a damn minute. His auntie let his ex

move up into her house?"

Carmen nodded her head. "Yeah. I don't understand it myself, and neither does Kevin. His ex isn't exactly one of Mrs. Ridley's favorite people."

"You need to keep your eyes on that girl, Carmen. Something sounds really suspicious about all of that."

"Yeah. I know. That's exactly what I was thinking. I could tell from the way she kept looking at me out the side of her eye, that she don't like me. Based on the way Kevin said she treated him when they were married — the cheating and whatnot — the feeling's about to be mutual."

"Girl, y'all gonna be living together — at least for the next few months. If she eva do anything sketchy, hit me up. Imma roll over there and we gone treat her ass to a beatdown. Excuse me Jesus for saying a cuss word."

Carmen couldn't help but smile at that last little part. *Lord, bless my bestie's little heart.*

Over in Dominique's New Room at Halo House:

When she heard somebody knocking on her door, Dominique got up from sitting on her bed. Since she didn't know anybody at Halo House besides Janelle and the Ridleys, she figured it was one of them knocking. Sure enough, it was Janelle.

Janelle looked sneakily over both her shoulders. She didn't want anybody seeing her going into Dominique's room — that would've looked suspicious.

"Come on in, my friend."

Janelle took one more look, then stepped into the room.

Dominique smiled. "You my first visitor, girl. Come in. Have a seat. I *would* offer you some snacks or shit, but I ain't got a mini fridge or nothing."

Janelle nodded her head. "Don't worry about all that. How did things go downstairs between you and your husband. I heard through the grapevine that y'all talked."

A nasty look overtook Dominique's otherwise beautiful face. "Then you must've heard that he got himself engaged to that trick."

Janelle frowned. "Yeah. I heard that too. But you and Kevin belong together. So you really ain't gotta worry about all of that. You just have to play your cards like we talked about that day I got you out that trap house and into rehab."

Dominique still loved Kevin. She may have stepped out on him a couple of times, but she still felt like he was the man for her. She shook her head in disappointment. "I don't really see how our plan's gonna work, Janelle. It ain't like Kevin lives here. How am I gonna be able to seduce him and remind him of our good times."

"He be here often enough. At least three or four times a week, helping his uncle around this m-f'er." Her eyes finally met Dominique's. "Don't tell me you don't know how to seduce a man. I know your ass been out there tricking and some of er'thing else to get your next drug fix. I'm sure plenty of men probably wanted to hit it in exchange for them paying for your heroin or whatever other shit you was smoking."

Dominique felt offended. She frowned at Janelle. "Don't worry about me and whether or not I know how to seduce a man, Janelle. You need to be worrying about yourself. You in love with Carmen. But it don't look like to me she the type who gonna be interested in bedding herself down with no woman...with no lesbo."

Janelle smiled. "You let me worry about, Carmen. After your husband leaves her ass and breaks her heart, she gone be down for whateva." She rubbed her hands together, as if she was anticipating a tasty treat. "Imma swoop right in and pick up all them pieces. Them some facts right there."

*C*HAPTER 10

Carmen couldn't remember a time in her life when she'd been happier. She was going to marry the brotha of her dreams in three short months. She'd thought about them marrying sooner, but in the end, she'd decided she wanted to be completely free of the court system when they exchanged their 'I do's'. She wanted them to be able to go away on location for their honeymoon...she wanted to go to the Bahamas. The terms of her parole wouldn't allow that until her six-month tenure at Halo House was completed.

As for Dominique, it was more than evident to Carmen that the chick didn't like her. She knew that her relationship with Kevin had everything to do with that. It was clearly evident that Dominique was salty about Kevin and Carmen being engaged.

Just like now. Despite having a full-time job, Carmen still did chores around Halo House. She'd just gotten finished wiping down one of the bathrooms when Dominique walked past her and sucked her teeth. "You missed a spot, Carmen. I feel sorry for Kevin's ass. I used to keep our house clean. I'm talking spotless. If y'all hook up, he gonna be living in a pigsty."

Carmen knew that the girl was saying what she'd said just to try to to get on her nerves. So Carmen refused to take the bait. "I think the bathroom downstairs needs cleaning, Dominique. How about you handle that? We can compare our work. It ain't like you're doing too much around here anyways."

Dominique sucked her teeth again. "Whatever." Then she walked away.

As she made her way back to her room, Dominique started thinking about the reason why she'd come to Halo House in the first place. She'd been there two weeks, and she had yet to get any alone time with Kevin. Every time he came to the house, Carmen would be all up in his face.

Two days later, she finally got the opportunity that she'd been waiting on. Carmen's friend, Lisa, had just picked her up. The two had walked out of the house talking about how they were going to spend the whole afternoon together. Kevin had rolled up a half hour later.

Dominique flew up the stairs and changed out of the clothes she'd been wearing. Since she'd been cleaning the house, she'd had on an old T-shirt and sweatpants — she hadn't wanted to clean anything though, she'd just gotten tired of hearing Mrs. Ridley complaining about her doing nothing.

Since she knew that Kevin liked seeing her in dresses, she slipped on a sexy little number that she'd talked Janelle into buying for her. It hit her mid thigh, and she knew she looked good in it.

Kevin was changing out a wall switch in the upstairs hallway when Dominique walked up to him and whispered in a sexy little voice, "Hey, husband. How you feeling today?"

Kevin caught a whiff of the perfume that he'd liked smelling on Dominique. He'd even bought her a bottle or two of the old-school fragrance — Eternity by Calvin Klein — in the past...when they'd been married. The scent repulsed him now.

"Yeah, it's me, Kevin." Dominique winked her eye. "You can talk to me now...you know, since Carmen's gone out the house for the day."

Kevin didn't feel like dealing with his ex, but he decided to be cordial. "Afternoon, Dominique."

She laughed. "You remember that day you replaced the wall plates at our house, Kevin? You weren't even able to finish because we decided to get freaky right there in the kitchen?" She licked her lips. "That was some good sex that day...wasn't it?"

Kevin didn't feel like going there with his ex-wife. He'd lost all the respect that he'd had for Dominique a long, long time ago.

She wouldn't let it drop. "I know you remember, Kevin." She got up close to him. "I had on the very same perfume that I'm wearing now. And I sprayed it right wear you used to like me spraying it, too." She placed her hand between her thighs to jog his memory.

He finally frowned. "How about quit it, Dominique. We're not married anymore. It's inappropriate for you to be talking to me like that. It ain't right."

Dominique didn't pay his words any attention. She had her prey in her crosshairs and she intended on moving out on the hunt. She reached up her nether regions and snatched off her panties. She twirled them on one finger then tossed them on Kevin's head. She laughed. "I bet your ass remember that smell don't you?"

Mrs. Ridley opened her bedroom door and caught the tail end of what had just been going on. Standing there with a pair of pink panties on his head, Kevin felt both angry and embarrassed. He knew that everything looked incriminating. However, his auntie zeroed her line of vision right on Dominique. "You need to take your nasty drawers and yourself back to your room and put on some real clothes, little girl. Then you need to focus yourself on leaving my nephew alone. Y'all ain't married no more... You hear?"

Dominique laughed. "You just mad 'cause ain't nobody wanting your panties no more, old woman."

Michelle narrowed her eyes. "God don't like ugly, Dominique. Keep playing with his people, and you'll see."

By this time, Kevin had moved his head downwards, thus depositing Dominique's panties on the floor. Dominique bent down and scooped them up. Then she made her way back to her own room.

Michelle shook her head and looked at the grown man that she'd helped raise. "I know you're smart enough not to get yourself caught back up with Dominique, Kevin. You and Carmen got a good thing going for yourselves."

Kevin nodded. "Yes, ma'am, Aunt Michelle."

In Dominique's eyes, her little interaction with her ex-husband had been a score. She could've sworn that she'd seen the light of interest in his sexy, bedroom eyes.

She flopped down on her bed on her back, spread-eagle. "He still wants me. I don't give a damn about that expensive ring Carmen's flashing on her finger. Me and my man are getting back together. It's only gonna be a matter of time."

Dominique suddenly had an idea. *Wait a minute, maybe I was going about things all wrong a few minutes ago. Kevin's obviously taking this Jesus phase of his life seriously. I need to step to him a little differently.*

She slipped out of her dress and pulled on some baggy jeans and a T-shirt. Then she went back out into the hallway.

"Hey again, Kevin. I'm glad you didn't leave yet. Look, I want to apologize for my behavior a few minutes ago. I thought about it, and I was wrong." She sighed for emphasis, then continued speaking. "As you probably already know, the last few years have been pretty rough for me. When I saw you out here today, I couldn't help but reflect back on when things in my life were right. When things were good." She smiled. "You were a big part of all of that. So yeah, I'm sorry for acting out a few minutes ago. It was totally unacceptable behavior."

Dominique sounded genuine to Kevin. So he gave her a genuine smile, nodded his head, and said, "I think I understand, Dominique. Apology accepted."

Yep, he fell for it, she thought to herself. *This is definitely the way to play him. Before I know it, we're gonna be back together. Besides getting myself hooked on drugs, letting Kevin go was my biggest mistake ever.*

She placed an innocent look on her face, then glanced down at the floor. "I guess I'll see you around, Kevin."

Kevin nodded his head. "Alright, Dominique."

Dominique made her way back to her room. She figured that that had gone really well. Now she had another trick up her sleeve.

I think it's time for me to work on my relationship with the Lord. She smiled to herself. *I'm about to start showing up at that church that Carmen and Kevin be going to every Sunday. I'm gonna have even more face time with him that way. Like they say: Outta sight, outta mind.* She shook her head. *I'm not about to let him all the way out of my sight.*

<<<<<>>>>

Across Town at the Mall:

Carmen and Lisa took a break from their window shopping at the mall. They decided to get in line and get themselves a couple of bubble teas. They paid for their drinks and found themselves a table in the food court. Lisa said a quick prayer over there teas, causing Carmen to smile. She'd never run into anyone who stopped to bless their drinks. Carmen always blessed her food — ever since she'd gotten saved — but never just her drinks.

Lisa said amen. Then she looked Carmen in the eye. "Girl, yes...I most definitely *did* go there. I'm grateful to God for everything. So I have to bless him for everything that he's done for my sinful behind."

Carmen nodded her head. "I hear you, boo."

"Most definitely. Now on a different subject, how are things going for you over at Halo House? Is Dominique still acting crazy? Or did her butt decide to start playing it cool?"

Carmen shook her head. "Girl, don't even get me started on all of that. We just might be here all day if I do."

"So she's still acting crazy."

"Yep. I don't pay her any attention most of the time. I just keep praying on it. I have to believe that God'll handle it all."

"I'm sure God'll handle it. But so would a good old-fashioned beatdown. I'm still leaning towards that beatdown you know?"

Carmen laughed. "You're a mess, Lisa. But it's good to know that my girl's got my back."

Later on that night, Kevin took his bath and got ready for bed. He made it a point to speak to Carmen on the phone every night. It was their routine. He would call, and they'd stay on the phone for at least an hour.

He grabbed his phone and laid down on top of his comforter. He smiled. *Once we tie the knot, I'm gonna have my baby here with me in the flesh. We won't have to worry about calling each other to say good night.* He thought of how physically attracted he was to his fiancée. *We'll still tell each other goodnight, but it'll be in another way.*

He suddenly got to thinking back over his day. His

mind landed on the stunt that Dominique had tried to pull. Then he thought about how she'd suddenly decided to correct herself. He didn't have any hate in his heart for Dominique — he really did wish her the best — so he said a quick prayer for her. As a true Christian, it was Kevin's desire that every person developed their very own positive relationship with Christ.

"Lord, bless her," he whispered. "Her life really will change for the better if she allows you into her heart."

He pushed his thoughts about his ex out of his mind, and placed them on his future — on Carmen. He smiled. *My beautiful brown-skinned Cinderella is my everything. I can't wait to see her lovely face tomorrow morning in church.*

The Next Day:

Carmen and Kevin arrived for services at Calvary Christian Center a little early. Needless to say, they were both surprised when Dominique walked into the sanctuary. Kevin was proud of Dominique for deciding to come to church. Carmen, on the other hand, was suspicious. *Something just ain't right with this here picture. I'm all for people coming to Christ, but something doesn't feel legit about all of this. It's something about her spirit. I can feel it way over here.*

At the end of the church service, the pastor did his altar call. He asked anyone in the congregation who was interested in receiving Jesus to come up to the front of the church so that he could pray for them and begin the process of them accepting Christ into their lives. Dominique was the very first person to go up to that altar.

Normally, Carmen would be the last person to knock someone getting their walk with God on. But she felt like Dominique was faking. *Lord, just look at this right here.* She shook her head, then sighed. *At the end of the day, that's between her and God. It ain't none of my business. Just as long as she leaves me and my man alone, Imma leave her butt alone.*

Fifteen minutes later as Carmen and Kevin were leaving the church's parking lot, Kevin reached across the center console and gave Carmen's hand a little squeeze. "It was a good service today...huh, babe? The spirit of the Lord was all up in the building."

Carmen smiled. She nodded her head. "Yep. I could definitely feel it."

"And it was great how Dominique decided to go ahead and give her life over to the Lord. We're not married anymore, so I don't have a connection to her like that, but I'm always excited when somebody who's been living a life like Dominique turns over a new leaf. It was a powerful thing."

151

Carmen was trying her best not to be affected by her fiancé's words, but she couldn't help herself. A spirit that she wasn't used to feeling — jealousy — rose up like bile in her throat. She was ashamed of feeling like that. But try as she may, she couldn't totally get rid of it.

She finally sighed and said, "Yeah, it's always good when somebody decides to give their life over to Christ." She brought her eyebrows together in a frown. "But do you think she was for real, babe?"

Kevin nodded his head. "Yeah...it seemed real to me. What reason could she possibly have to be faking? What is she gonna gain from doing that?"

Yeah, Carmen thought to herself. *That right there is the million dollar question*. She decided to leave all of that alone. She refused to allow Dominique to ruin her day with her man without her even being there.

Kevin's aunt, Michelle, regularly attended a church across town from the one that Carmen and Kevin had just stepped out of. Since her husband, Nathan, had decided to stay home that day due to trouble with his bad back, Michelle had gone to services with her lifelong best friend, Deidre McFadden.

Services had just ended for them too, so Deidre and Michelle were leaving their house of worship.

Deidra turned around in her passenger-side seat and looked at her bestie. "So...how are things going with Dominique up in your house, girl?"

Michelle frowned. "Honey, don't even get me started. You won't believe it. Yesterday, her little narrow behind was trying to flirt with Kevin. Now she know they're over with...that he done moved on...that he's getting married to Carmen. But did that make any difference to her?" She answered her own question. "No, it most certainly didn't."

Michelle shook her head in disgust. "I just wish I could kick her behind out my house. I know she up to no good."

"You should gone head and do it, Michelle."

Michelle sighed. "You know I can't, Deidre. You're my bestie. You're like a sister to me. You know all my secrets. You know exactly what's at stake if I do that. That girl is gonna open her big, fat mouth, and ruin my family."

"Pastor Lee took his Scripture for today from Luke 8 and 17: *For there is nothing hidden that will not be disclosed, and nothing concealed that will not be be known or brought out into the open*." Deidre paused for but a moment to let her words sink in. Then she added, "I think that Scripture was especially for you, Michelle. I think it's probably time for you to come clean, honey...way past time."

Deidre sighed then continued speaking. "Besides,

everybody who's affected by that secret that you're carrying is full grown now. Everybody should be more than able to handle it coming out into the open. But I'm gonna leave that alone. In the end, that decision is up to you."

Michelle grimaced again. *Some secrets should be taken to the grave. I think this here is one of them. In the meantime, I'm gonna have to keep praying to God that he won't allow that heifer to cause trouble for my husband's only biological son, my sister's only biological son...for Kevin.*

That was the secret that Michelle intended to take to her grave. Her husband wasn't Kevin's uncle, he was really his father — the result of a drunken one-night stand her sister and her husband had had thirty-five years ago.

Kevin's aunt and uncle hadn't been married back when that one night stand had taken place — they didn't fall in love until much later. But her sister had been married to a man named, Eric. Michelle's sister, Brenda, had known that her husband would leave her if he found out the truth. She'd told Michelle everything one day and Michelle had agreed to keep her secret.

My husband will never forgive me for hiding something like this from him. Neither will Kevin. Besides my sister, Brenda, the two of them are my closest living relatives. I can't let this come out. They can't know that I knew the truth all along. Imma have to find some kind of way to deal with Dominique. She's threatening everything that's dear to me.

"Did you hear me, Michelle?"

Michelle pulled herself out of her thoughts. "What did you say, Deidre?"

"You just missed your exit."

Michelle frowned. "Oh. Sorry about that, honey. I guess I wasn't paying attention. I'll take the next one."

In her head, Deidre said a quick prayer for her best friend. Something was telling her that all hell was about to break loose. *I'm just praying that my bestie and her family makes it safely through the fallout.*

<<<<<>>>>>

Fifteen Minutes Later:

Kevin tucked Carmen's elbow under his hand and escorted her into the restaurant where they'd be having dinner that day. After their waiter had seated them, he turned to her and smiled. "Baby, once again, you were killing it today in that green dress. Absolutely gorgeous."

Carmen blushed. She loved getting compliments from her man. "Thank you, sweetheart."

They had only been in the restaurant five minutes when Dominique walked through the door and was seated at the table across from theirs.

Oh no she didn't, Carmen thought to herself.

Carmen didn't think Dominique suddenly appearing there was a coincidence. *This trick is somehow following us. I know it.*

Dominique flashed Kevin a smile and waved at both him and his fiancée. "Hey, you two. Good food that they have here... Huh?"

Carmen refused to act other than herself. She simply nodded her head at her fiancé's ex-wife and said, "Very good."

Carmen normally enjoyed her and Kevin's Sunday outings. However, Dominique's presence made that impossible this particular Sabbath.

This is a test, Lord, Carmen thought to herself. *That's what this is. You're trying to see whether or not Imma hold on to my salvation. The old me would've been done hopped over there in that girl's face. I would've been warning her off of my man...probably about ready to fight. But that's not your way. That's not how you want your people acting. If I say I'm saved, it should show in my behavior. This is most definitely a test.*

"You okay, sweetheart?"

Carmen smiled at her fiancé. She wasn't going to give Dominique anymore thought while they were in the restaurant enjoying their time together. She intended to stomp the devil and all his tricks and deceptions under her feet. "Yeah, babe. I'm fine. Just as long as we're together, I'm right as rain."

When Dominique finally laid her head on her pillow at a little past ten that night, she had a triumphant little smile on her face. "That little act I put on over at that church sure pulled the wool over Kevin's eyes. That nigga gullible...he believed all of it. But I love his ass. It won't be long till he's all mine again."

CHAPTER 11

The next week passed by slowly for Carmen. That's because she'd caught some type of bug and had been a little under the weather. But she hadn't been down for long. A lot of that had to do with Janelle insisting on fixing Carmen some special chicken soup. That soup had made Carmen feel a whole lot better.

Despite the fact that Janelle lived a different lifestyle than Carmen, Carmen was still happy to be able to call Janelle her friend. Janelle was always doing something to make Carmen's day a little easier, and Carmen appreciated her for that.

Janelle knocked on Carmen's room door and stepped inside as soon as she told her to come in. "Hey, Carmen. The Farmer's Market had these cherries on sale. I know how much you love 'em. So I bought you some."

Carmen smiled. "Thank you, Janelle." Then she went over to her closet and pulled an item out. "And I got something for you, too. This was on sale at the mall. I know it's your team. I wouldn't be a real friend if I'd left it on the rack."

Janelle took the Pistons jersey from the girl that she'd fallen in love with. She smiled. "Awwww. Thank you, boo. I didn't think you cared." She pretended to dab at imaginary tears on her cheeks.

Carmen laughed. "Girl, please. We gonna be friends for life. I can tell."

Yep, Janelle liked hearing that. She hoped the day never came when she wouldn't get to see Carmen. "Hug on it, friend?"

Carmen smiled. "Of course, girl."

Janelle made the hug real brief — after all, she wasn't ready for Carmen to know how she was feeling about her just yet. She wanted to hold Carmen in her arms for ever. She found solace in the fact that she knew their day was coming.

"See you later, Carmen. Work is calling my name again."

"Alright, girl."

After Janelle had left, Carmen began thinking over what her bestie, Lisa, kept telling her. Lisa kept saying there was something about Janelle that she didn't trust. She couldn't quite put her finger on it, but she kept saying she knew something sketchy was there.

Janelle's a sweetheart. Yes, she's gay and I know the Bible says that's wrong. But that's between her and God. That girl has been good to me. She's been a real friend.

159

Carmen decided to move on from thinking about all of that. Kevin would be there to pick her up any minute and she didn't want to be late. She looked out her window to see if he'd arrived yet. Sure enough, he was pulling up in his truck.

She frowned when she saw him. She couldn't understand why both of his vehicles were now parked out there along the curb.

She made her way downstairs and out the front door. "Hey, Bae. What's up with both of your cars being here?"

Kevin smiled. Then he pulled his fiancée into his arms for a hug and a quick kiss. "Good morning to you, too, sweetheart." Then he pulled back, reached into his pocket, and handed her a single key on a key ring. "The Beemer's all yours, Carmen. I only drive it for special occasions and on Sundays. Other than that, I drive my truck. We can go put your name on the title next week."

Needless to say, Carmen was shocked. Her eyes grew wide in surprise. "You're giving me the BMW? You're signing your baby over to me?"

He nodded his head. He laughed. "Yeah. She's all yours, sweetheart." His eyes met hers. "You *do* want the Beemer, don't you, Carmen? Since I love you so much, I'll give you the truck if that's what you really want."

Carmen wanted the BMW alright. Ever since she'd

gotten out of prison, she'd been without a car. Being without a vehicle made getting around town, and to the other places she needed to go to, an inconvenience. "Are you sure, Bae?"

He nodded his head. "Just as sure as I am about my name being Kevin. And before you try to refuse, we *are* going to be married in a few months. So I don't really see why you should be turning the car down. I'm the type of man who likes taking care of his woman." He shook his head. "I can't have you out there walking the streets of Atlanta and riding the buses at all times of the night. What kind of man would I be if I did something like that?"

Everything he was telling her made perfect sense to Carmen. She finally nodded her head. She smiled. "Thank you, sweetheart. You're too good to me, Kevin. How am I ever going to repay you for this?"

He wrapped his arms around her waist again. "You've already paid me, Carmen. You agreed to become my wife." He grinned again. "Now...are you ready to chauffeur me around town for the day in your new car?"

"Yeah. I'm down for that."

Inside the downstairs study of Halo House, Dominique was sitting in a chair right beside an open window. She had a good pair of ears, so she heard Kevin and Carmen's entire conversation. Her ex had given Carmen his expensive car — she definitely didn't like that.

A fierce scowl made its way onto Dominique's pretty face. *Things have been moving along pretty good between Kevin and I so far. With my newfound fake love of Jesus, he's starting to accept me a little bit more. But it's time to up the ante now—*, she finally smiled, *—and I know exactly what to do to accomplish that.*

She got up from her seat and made her way to the kitchen. It was time to start on the other part of her plan. This part involved Kevin's aunt, Mrs. Ridley.

Dominique took a deep breath and placed a suitable repentant expression on her face. Then she walked into the kitchen.

"Morning, Mrs. Ridley. Can I talk to you in private for a few minutes."

Michelle frowned at Dominique. She had no desire to speak to her about anything. All she really wanted was for the girl to be out of all of their lives. "What do you want, little girl?"

Dominique forced herself to lift her lips in a tiny little smile. "I've been doing some soul searching. I wanna apologize to you for some things."

Mrs. Ridley's frown didn't go anywhere. Deciding to hear Dominique out, she wiped her hands on a tea towel and said, "We can talk in my bedroom. Nobody's in there."

A few minutes later, Mrs. Ridley had listened to

what Dominique had had to say. She'd apologized for threatening to blow the cover on Mrs. Ridley's secret. The middle-aged woman had thanked her for her apology, but she didn't believe Dominique.

Seconds after Dominique left her bedroom, Mrs. Ridley shook her head. "I don't trust that girl. Her sinful behind is up to something. I don't care how touched by Jesus she's claiming to be."

Dominique, on the other hand, had thought that the meeting with Mrs. Ridley had gone really well. She didn't need the woman as an enemy. *Especially now that I intend on being a member of this family again. Kevin loves his auntie—*, she frowned, *—only God knows why. My ass gonna have to get used to playing nice towards her.*

She then pushed all of her thoughts about Mrs. Ridley out of her mind. She smiled. She was ready to escalate her plan on getting Kevin.

<<<<<>>>>>

Kevin believed in giving back to his community, so he volunteered at his church as one of the teachers in their GED program for adults. The class was normally offered on Tuesday and Thursday evenings from six-thirty to eight.

He parked his truck in the lot of Cornerstone Baptist. Then he made his way into the conference room where the class was being held. The first order of the evening was to check his log of attendees. All the normal names he was expecting to be there were indeed on his roster. The name of the newest participant who'd just signed up, shocked him. *Dominique Y Parker*.

He shook his head. *No, it can't be*. As soon as he'd had that thought, his ex-wife walked into the room.

"Hey, teacher. After all these years, do you believe I'm finally taking your advice? Do you believe I'm shooting for my GED?"

Kevin gave his ex-wife a sincere smile. "I'm glad you decided to take this step, Dominique. You're gonna be able to go a lot further in life with an education."

That hadn't been the reason why Dominique had signed up for the GED class. She'd signed up so that she could get more face time with Kevin. But she nodded her head and said, "Lord knows that's the truth. I prayed on it and prayed on it. God told me in a dream that I had last week to do it."

She smiled again. "But I didn't know you were gonna be instructing the class." *That had totally been a lie*. "I hope Carmen's not gonna be upset that I'm in here. You guys are some of the only people offering the course for free. I don't have a job yet. The average going price for these classes are $20 a week. I couldn't afford that."

"All are welcome here, Dominique. Have a seat.

You're a little early, but the room should be filling up in about twenty minutes or so."

Dominique went out of her way to chit-chat with Kevin for as much of those twenty minutes as possible. By the end of the evening, she was convinced that signing up for the class had been her best move yet.

She purposely hung around until everyone else besides herself and Kevin had left the building. Then she approached him and said, "I hate to bother you, Kevin. But I only have twenty-five cents to my name right now. I walked over here. I was hoping that maybe you could drop me back off at Halo House."

Kevin didn't really feel like doing that. However, he knew that Dominique had to walk through a dicey part of town that was only a few feet from some of the trap houses that she'd used to frequent. *I'll feel guilty if she starts walking home right now and decides to take a detour to one of those drug paradises. She worked so hard on getting herself clean. Making sure she gets to Halo House is the Godly things for me to do.*

He nodded his head. "Alright, Dominique. I'll be ready to go in five minutes."

She smiled again. "Okay."

<<<<<>>>>>

Carmen knew what Kevin's truck sounded like. The

minute she heard him pulling up to Halo House, she looked out her window. The sun had just set, so it was dark outside. But she could clearly see who had just gotten out of his Ford F-350.

Why is that trick riding around town with my freaking man? Yep, Carmen was definitely hot about that. So hot in fact, that she didn't even go downstairs to investigate what was going on. She was scared she was gonna lose her religion and scalp Dominique.

Fuming upstairs in her room, Carmen nodded her head. *His butt's gonna call me tonight. Imma see what he has to say about all of this. I'm gonna see if he brings it up himself, or if I have to drag it out of him.*

Kevin called Carmen at exactly ten-thirty that evening, like he always did. She pretended like everything was perfectly fine. However, after they'd been talking for ten minutes and he still hadn't brought up his ex-wife, she was starting to get a whole lot of salty.

When he finally said — *"Bae, you're not gonna believe it, but Dominique signed up for my GED class. She asked me to drop her off at Halo House tonight, and I did"* — Carmen released a sigh of relief.

Thank you Lord, she thought to herself. *He's not trying to hide anything from me*. Despite having that thought, Carmen said, "I'm gonna be upfront and honest with you, babe. I don't trust you ex. Especially not around you. I think she wants you back."

Kevin didn't think that was the case at all. "I don't think so, sweetheart."

"But I do. I don't think all these instances of her being all up in your face are coincidental. In other words, I think she planned all of it. From being up in Halo House, to being up in your GED class right now as we speak. I think she strategically orchestrated all of that."

"She's in both Halo House and my GED class out of necessity, babe." He chuckled. "I don't think she has some grand scheme that she's working on to get me back or something."

Carmen wasn't backing down. "But I do. And I think you need to recognize that."

"You *do* understand how big of an accomplishment it was that she was actually able to get herself clean, don't you?" He sighed. "You recognize the importance of having a good education, that's why you got yourself certified to take the bar exam. So I know you understand how much of a positive impact having a GED will have all Dominique's life."

Despite trying to be civil about everything, Carmen felt herself getting angry all over again. "What I don't understand is why my fiancé has to be involved in any of it. And what I really, really don't understand is why he should care so much about it."

Carmen knew that her comments were being

167

fueled by jealousy. But she hadn't been able to stop herself.

"Babe, I think you might be overreacting a tad bit."

"Overreacting my behind," she sneered. "If the tables were reversed, and it was me who had the ex-husband all up in my face, you wouldn't be singing that tune right now."

Kevin sighed. "Once again, I think you might be overreacting sweetheart."

Carmen didn't feel like saying what she'd said the first time all over again. She shook her head. She was upset. "Look, it's late, Kevin. I gotta go. I'll see you tomorrow at Pondfield."

Dominique was a real piece of work. Her room was right beside Carmen's and the walls were kind of thin. The second she'd heard Carmen's cell phone ring, she'd grabbed herself a cup. She'd proceeded to place both her cup and her ear to the thin wall, so that she could listen in on the entire conversation.

As soon as Carmen hung up on Kevin, Dominique cheesed like the Kool-Aid man himself. She'd only heard one side of the conversation — Carmen's side. But it hadn't taken much for her to guess everything that had been said. *My plan is definitely working. It's only gonna be a matter of time now. Kevin is my true love. We belong together. Ain't nothing stopping our 'being together' from happening. Not nothing. Not nobody.*

Over in Carmen's room, Carmen couldn't believed that she and her fiancé had just had their very first argument. And even worse, she couldn't believe that it had all been over his ex-wife.

Lord, you don't want your flock harboring hate in their hearts. Please don't allow me to start despising that girl. That's not the type of person I want to be. But this mess Dominique's trying to pull is making that real easy for me.

Carmen sighed and kneeled down by her bedside on her knees. She knew that prayer was necessary right now for her sanity. Because what she really felt like doing was going next door and popping Dominique in the face. She didn't like being disrespected.

She shook her head. *But in the end, it's Kevin's call. Not that thot's. Kevin is the one who made a commitment to me, not Dominique. So he should be the one standing by my side on all of this.*

The spirit between Kevin and Carmen had definitely changed after that little argument that fateful night. At work the day after it had happened, Carmen had refused to talk to Kevin — that is unless it had involved her job. Since Kevin had figured they needed a little cool down time between them, he'd let things be.

They were now rolling up on day three of their little disagreement and Kevin couldn't take his fiancée being angry at him anymore.

After the school day was over with, while still in his office, Kevin wrapped his hand gently around Carmen's forearm. He looked her in the eye. He frowned. "I can't take this spirit between us anymore, sweetheart. Two days of missing you are much too long. We need to talk."

Carmen felt the exact same way. She'd been hurt by the stance that her fiancé had chosen to take on his ex-wife. However, the pain from missing him was greater. So she was ready to talk about it. To work things out.

He continued speaking. "I was wrong. Mind you, Dominique hasn't done anything else suspicious. But you have every reason to be concerned."

He nodded his head. "And in response to your statement from that night... Yes, I'd be feeling the same way that you are right now if our roles were somehow reversed."

170

He placed his palm lightly against the side of her face. He caressed her cheek. "Do you forgive me, babe?"

Carmen finally smiled. As far as the problem with her fiancé was concerned, she'd chosen to stand on the wings of prayer. In other words, she'd decided to allow the Lord to handle it...in his way, in his time.

She nodded her head. "Yes, I do forgive you, sweetheart. Like the good book says in Matthew six and fifteen. If I don't forgive you, God won't forgive me." She winked her eye. "Plus, I've somehow developed a soft spot in my heart for your handsome behind." She playfully wagged her index finger at him. "But don't push it...you hear?"

He placed a sweet kiss on her lips. Then he pulled back and laughed, "I hear alright. And I'm glad I'm marrying a woman of strong faith. Real talk, I didn't know how much more of missing you I was gonna be able to take. You're like a drug that I've gotten myself addicted to, Carmen."

She smiled. "Good. Be sure to remember that the next time Dominique tries something." Her smile turned into a frown. "Because I'm sure she's not done yet. You can call that 'women's intuition'."

He took both of her hands into his. "Let me prayer over us, Bae."

Carmen was all for that. She felt abundantly blessed that she had a man who really believed in God in her life.

CHAPTER 12

Dominique was convinced that she was making progress with Kevin. She was working hard on her GED coursework. And she was making sure that she stayed over until everyone had left the classroom — all so that she and Kevin could get some extra time in to talk.

It had also become routine for Kevin to drop Dominique back off at Halo House once the class session was over with every Tuesday and Thursday evening.

Janelle, of course, had wanted frequent updates on the situation. She was glad that Dominique appeared to be making progress. However, she was ready for them to take things up a notch.

For privacy sake, Janelle and Dominique met at a Mickey D's one afternoon to discuss everything.

"I think it's time to nail the final coffin in Carmen and Kevin's little relationship," Janelle said.

Sitting in a booth in the very back of the McDonald's, Dominique frowned. "Things are going along just fine, Janelle. Things are starting to feel like old times between me and Kevin. I know he felt like kissing me day before yesterday. I could tell from the look in his eyes."

"That's all good, Dominique. But like I said, it's time to put an end to them being a couple."

"Alright. How do you propose we go about doing that?"

Janelle smiled. She began rubbing her hands together. "It's real simple. Make Carmen think y'all sleeping together."

"Now how am I supposed to do that?"

Janelle let out a breath on a sigh. "Damn, Dominique. Do I have to tell you how to do everything?"

Dominique frowned. "I know I don't have my GED yet. But you don't have to act like I'm stupid. I'm obviously just not as devious as you."

"Alright, alright... Ain't no need to be getting your pretty pink panties all in a bunch. Check it out. This is what Imma need you to do."

The plan seemed simple enough, so Dominique agreed to it. Janelle was going to break the wall outlet by Dominique's bed. When Kevin showed up to fix it, the plan was for Dominique to throw herself on him in a sensual type of way. Using her cell phone, Janelle was going to snap some pictures.

Janelle smiled. "See what I'm talking about now, baby girl? That's gonna be all she wrote. I been talking to Carmen, and she still don't trust you with her man. All it's gonna take is something like this to push her over the top. Then — being the wonderful friend that I am to her — I'm gonna step right in and tell her to leave his ass. Me and Carmen are tight like that. She's gonna listen. Then he'll be all yours, Dominique. And Carmen will be all mine."

Dominique grinned, too. "Okay, Janelle. I can handle that."

<<<<<>>>>>

Later on that Afternoon:

Kevin's aunt frowned as Dominique walked through the front door of Halo House. *That girl is playing like she's saved, playing like she's a changed woman. But I can sense that it's all lies. I don't trust her. She's about to ruin my family. She's holding that secret over my head and I can't stand it anymore.*

Mrs. Ridley didn't know what she was going to do about her problem with Dominique. But she knew she had to do something. *I can't let her do this to the people I love. Not my Nathan, not my Kevin...not to Carmen neither. That girl got hate in her heart for Carmen. I don't care how much she's pretending otherwise now. I can see it.*

Feeling good because she was sure everything was

175

about to turn in her favor, Dominique flashed Mrs. Ridley one of her brightest smiles. "I hope you had a blessed day today, Mrs. Ridley."

Two can play at this game, Mrs. Ridley thought to herself. She smiled right back at Dominique. "The Lord is keeping me, child."

Neither Dominique, nor Janelle wanted to wait to finally put their plan into motion. Therefore, Janelle broke the wall fixture in Dominique's room that very night. Dominique had told Mrs. Ridley about it with a quickness. According to her, Kevin would be coming over to fix it on the weekend — which was only two days away.

For Janelle, waiting for Saturday to arrive was like waiting on Christmas. She'd even taken the day off of work to ensure that her little plan went off without a hitch.

Janelle's cell phone was fully charged when Kevin made it to Halo House that Saturday morning. And to make the situation even better, Carmen had once again gone out with Lisa for the day — which had actually become a regular thing, so Janelle had been counting on it.

Janelle did a brief little knock on Dominique's room door. She stuck her head in the room and whispered, "Showtime."

Dominique smiled. She was more than ready. Ever since Janelle had come up with the plan two days ago, Dominique had been having nightly dreams about it. She couldn't wait to have Kevin back.

To make things look even better, she'd slipped on a little red dress that looked more like lingerie than daytime clothes.

"Go ahead and hide in the closet, Janelle," Dominique quietly hissed. "I can hear him walking up the stairs."

Out of respect, Kevin knocked on Dominique's open door. "Hey, Dominique. Michelle told me that your wall fixture needs fixing." He held up his toolbox. "I'm here to take care of that."

Dominique smiled. "Sure thing, Kevin. Come on in."

When Kevin felt Dominique's arms around him, and saw her face close to his, he'd only been in her room for less than a minute. It happened so quickly that he was shocked. Unfortunately, his state of shock gave Janelle all the time she needed to snap her photos from her hiding place in the closet.

Kevin extracted himself out of Dominique's clutches. He frowned. "I thought you had changed, Dominique," he said in disappointment. Then his anger took over. "I think Carmen was right."

Dominique had already played over in her mind how she was going to respond to him after she'd pulled her shenanigans.

She shook her head. "I'm so sorry, Kevin. I must have been misreading the signals you were sending me." She crossed her arms over her chest, pretending to protect her long-gone innocence.

She continued speaking. "With all the talking we been doing lately — all the getting along — things were starting to feel like old times to me between us. You know, when things were good? I suppose I was wrong. I'm sorry. And I'm so embarrassed. Look... I'm gonna get some real clothes out of my closet real quick, and then I'm going to take myself a walk. You don't have to run anywhere this time. You can stay and fix the wall fixture."

With that being said, she rushed over to her closet and pulled out jeans and a T-shirt. Well out of sight, Janelle gave her a thumbs-up.

"I'm gonna change my clothes in the bathroom in the hallway. Bye, Kevin."

As his ex-wife rushed out of her room, Kevin shook his head. *I guess my baby was right about Dominique still liking me. But at least my ex now understands that we don't have a snowball's chance in hell of being together. Not ever.*

He decided to go ahead and make the repair.

Carmen and Lisa both believed in keeping their bodies in shape. Therefore, they decided to start their day off at the gym. They'd claimed two treadmills that were side by side at Planet Fitness. When the notification popped up on Carmen's phone telling her that she had a new text message, they were walking along chatting about Carmen's upcoming wedding.

Carmen frowned at the unknown number. "Wait a second, boo. Let me see what this text message is all about."

Lisa laughed. "It's probably just your fiancé texting your lucky butt again." Lisa smiled. "You sure are blessed to have found Kevin, Carmen."

Carmen grinned, too. "Honey, that's what I be thinking every single day. And don't worry, your bestie's got your back. I've been praying that God'll place a good man in your life, too."

"Thank you, Carmen. That's why me and you are gonna be friends forever. We gonna be the black Golden Girls. I call Dorothy. You can be Sophia. We both too smart to be Rose. And not skanky enough to be Blanche."

Carmen laughed at that. But her laughter came to an abrupt halt and she almost fell off the treadmill, when she saw the picture that was attached to the text she'd just downloaded.

A look of concern came on Lisa's face. She pressed the button to stop her treadmill. "What's wrong, honey?"

Carmen didn't say a word. She couldn't. She handed her phone to her bestie.

"Oh, h to the naw. We 'bout to go kick both they asses. Then we gonna ask the Lord to forgive us after."

When Carmen walked through the front door of Halo House with puffy, red-tinged eyes, Mrs. Ridley knew that something was up. She didn't need to hear Carmen's friend, Lisa, fussing and shouting something about *'Where's Dominique'* to know that. Mrs. Ridley's eyes were full of concern when she grabbed Carmen by the arms. "What's wrong, child? What's done happened?"

Lisa was hot. She reached her hand into Carmen's purse and snatched out her cell phone. She pressed the button and put the phone into Mrs. Ridley's face. "What you need to be asking is what's wrong with that nephew of yours? This here picture is recent. It was taken right here in this house. I know cause all these guest rooms look alike."

Mrs. Ridley shook her head at the picture. "Lord have mercy. Lord have mercy," she whispered under her breath.

Angry, Lisa nodded her head. "Lord have mercy is exactly right. Cause Dominique and Kevin both gonna need the Lord when I get done with them!" She directed her attention to the stairs. She began hollering. "Come on down here, Dominique. Come on down here, you skank!"

Mrs. Ridley shook her head. "She left well over an hour ago. Said she was going for a walk. And Kevin — he left about ten minutes ago. He was up in Dominique's room fixing her wall socket."

Lisa snickered. "I bet his no-good behind was fixing her wall socket alright. Looks like to me, he was fixing way more than that." Lisa turned to her girl. "I'm staying here all day Carmen. We gonna wait for Dominique to get back."

Mrs. Ridley liked Carmen a whole lot. And she didn't want to see her getting into any trouble over what had just happened.

They had drawn a crowd of the other residents at the house by now, prompting Mrs. Ridley to shake her head. "I know your contract says you're supposed to stay here everyday, Carmen. But I think in this specific case we need to make an exception. Go spend the night with your friend here. Think over all of this and come back in the morning. Or even tomorrow evening."

Lisa had wanted to stay. But Carmen wanted to leave. She didn't really want to deal with Dominique right then. She couldn't rightly say what she was or wasn't going to do to the girl. Therefore, with her heartbroken, she went upstairs and packed herself an overnight bag. Then her and Lisa took off.

Later on that Night:

Dominique had ended up spending the day hanging out with Janelle celebrating. At around nine that evening, Janelle decided to go ahead and take the bus home. Dominique, on the other hand, wanted to hang out a little bit longer at a bar that they had stumbled upon. Dominique spent an hour in the bar, then she decided to take the bus back to Halo house.

As she was walking up the street towards her destination, she heard someone shout, "You bitch!" Then she heard a loud pop, pop, pop sound, followed by feeling a burning pain in her back. In disbelief that she'd actually been shot, she crumpled to the sidewalk. And for her, it was lights out.

Across Town:

Carmen felt bad because of Kevin's act of deception. Since what she really needed was some alone time, and because Lisa was still living with her mother, Carmen asked her girl if she would take her back to Halo House. She'd be able to cry in peace there.

Carmen had prayed and was sure that she wasn't going to touch Dominique. She refused to break the terms of her parole and go back to jail over the girl.

Needless to say, she was surprised the next day when Atlanta's finest rolled up to Halo House looking for her.

Carmen took a seat in the study and began wringing her hands together. "What do you guys need to see me for, officers?"

Officer McManus looked Carmen directly in the eye. "Where were you last night at around 10 o'clock, ma'am?"

"Well, my best friend, Lisa, was driving me over here from her house at about that time."

"And she can vouch for you on that?"

Carmen nodded her head. "Yes. Most definitely. Look, am I in trouble or something, officer? What is this all about?"

He didn't answer her question. He asked one of his own. "I understand you had an altercation with Dominique Parker yesterday."

Carmen shook her head. "No, I didn't. I didn't see Dominique at all in person yesterday. Once again...am I under investigation or something, officer?"

"Not yet, Ms. Flood. Dominique Parker was shot last night. She's in a coma over at Grady. We were just trying to find out who did it."

Carmen felt as if the walls were crowding in on her. *They think I tried to kill her. I'm in big trouble now.*

The two officers stood up. "You've been in court before. This isn't your first rodeo. I know you realize you shouldn't leave town."

As soon as the officers left, Carmen went upstairs and laid on her bed. "Everything's going wrong, Lord. I don't understand it. First Kevin cheats on me. Now this."

She was worried. She needed some moral and psychological support before she completely lost it. So she picked up her phone to call her bestie, hoping to get some words of encouragement from her. Before she could dial Lisa's number, she noticed that she had several messages from the previous day. All Kevin of course, seeing that she wasn't answering his phone calls. She hadn't felt like talking to him.

I should just delete him from my whole phone, she thought angrily to herself. Then she recalled that they worked together, so she'd be seeing him again — and very soon at that.

She clicked on his first unanswered message and began reading it: *Carmen, I can't wait to see your pretty face. You won't believe what Dominique's done now. You were right all along. She never stopped*

184

carrying a flame for me. Threw herself at me today at Halo House. Tried to kiss me while wearing lingerie. I shut her down.

Carmen couldn't believe what she'd just read. She checked the time on the message. It had been sent to her before the picture had. She realized that her man was most likely telling her the truth.

A smile as bright as the sun materialized on her face. "I should've believed him. I shouldn't have jumped to my own conclusion based on an unknown source. I should've given him a chance to explain."

At that moment, she heard the familiar sound of his F-350's engine in the driveway. She flew off her bed and down the stairs. She pulled open the front door before he could even ring the doorbell.

"Sweetheart. I just got finished talking to Aunt Michelle. She told me what you think happened. It's all lies—"

She didn't let him finish his words. She pulled him into her arms, got on her tiptoes, and treated him to a scorching, toe-curling kiss.

He hadn't been expecting all of that. He'd thought that he was gonna have to plead his case. But he wasn't complaining. He accepted all the love that his woman was showering down on him.

Carmen pulled back and smiled. "I know you're innocent, babe. Sorry I didn't believe you at first. Next time, I'll come to you and let you explain. Okay?"

He grinned, too. He nodded his head. "By the grace of God, there won't be a next time. Hopefully, Dominique will leave us alone now."

Him mentioning Dominique's name made Carmen frown. She began to recall her latest problem. And it was a big one.

"What's wrong, sweetheart?"

"It's Dominique. She's been shot. She's in a coma over at Grady, and the police think I had something to do with it. I believe they think I did it."

Kevin frowned. "We're gonna have to get you a lawyer, babe. A real good one. Things aren't gonna go down like they did the first time for you."

Carmen appreciated how Kevin had immediately assumed she was innocent. She nodded her head. "Okay."

Over at Grady Memorial, Dominique was slowly coming out of her coma. She knew she was in the hospital but she couldn't quite remember why. She began to focus a little harder and the memories began flooding back into her brain. *I was shot, and I know who did it.*

A half hour later, her doctors had done another assessment of her situation. They'd told her that now that she'd awakened, they were a hundred percent certain that she'd make a recovery. However, since she couldn't feel anything below her knees, they weren't sure if she'd ever walk again. Dominique was distraught over that.

Her mind immediately went on Kevin. *I love him but I'm never gonna be able to have him again. I realize that now. Carmen's stole his heart. That sanctified skank stole my husband's heart. She may break up with him over those pictures, but he's never ever gonna come back to me. He said she's his damn soulmate. In all the years we were married, he never said that to me. He never said I was his soulmate.*

Two hours later, the authorities came in her room to question her about what had happened. Officer McManus looked Dominique in the eye. "Do you know who shot you, ma'am?"

Dominique nodded her head. "It was Carmen. I think her last name is Flood. She's my ex husband's new fiancé. She did this to me. She lives where I live at Halo House."

CHAPTER 13

Being locked up in a cell again felt surreal to Carmen. When she'd first been released months ago, she'd thought she'd never see the inside of lockdown again. But here she stood.

As a result of Dominique's statement, the police had come and picked Carmen up from church. It had been embarrassing and distressing. For both her and Kevin.

Kevin had promised her that she wouldn't be in jail for long. He'd said that he'd found her an attorney.

She'd only been locked up for four hours so far. She knew it was a Sunday. But she was hoping that between her attorney and Kevin, she'd be able to post bail and go home. However, she seriously doubted it, because the new accusations against her meant that she'd broken the terms of her parole.

The warden came and began opening the door to Carmen's cell. The man gave her an almost smile.
"You must know some people in some high places. Most folks ain't able to get sprung out of here like this on a Sunday. He looked down at her paperwork. "And

for attempted murder too... And while you're still on parole..."

Carmen frowned. "Yeah. I know some people in high places alright."

"Who?"

"Jesus Christ. That's who. Jesus Christ and God. That's who I know."

The man chuckled. "Oh, you're one of those — a Holy Roller. I guess you gonna be telling me next that you're innocent."

Carmen nodded her head. "I am. And I have faith that somehow, some way...my God is gonna prove that to the whole world. He's gonna show out and I'm gonna be free of these charges."

The warden chuckled. "Well amen to that Ms. Thang. Gone wit yo bad self."

A half hour later, Carmen's paperwork was completed and she was back in her man's arms.

Kevin opened the door of his truck and helped Carmen inside. Then he climbed into the driver's seat and took her hand into his. "I told you I'd get you out today, Bae. Lamont worked his wonders — he's a class 'A' attorney. And he's gonna work even more wonders if this case ends up going to trial. But I'm praying that it doesn't."

Carmen had talked to Kevin's attorney friend, Lamont, earlier that day. He'd been impressed by her grasp of the law, so he hadn't been surprised at all when he'd found out that she was studying to take the bar.

Carmen sighed. "I know the odds are stacked against me right now, babe. But like you said, good representation makes all the difference. I've found that to be true from my studies. So thank you for calling your friend."

Back at Halo House, Janelle was floored that Carmen had gotten locked up. And she was tee'd off that Dominique had claimed that she'd shot her. Janelle knew all of that wasn't the truth.

A look of determination came on Janelle's face. She grabbed her Pistons hat from out of her closet and hit the street. *I have to make this right for my boo.*

An hour later, she was downtown at the central police station talking to Officer McManus.

"So you're telling me that you're pretty much sure that Carmen Flood wasn't the one who shot Dominique Parker, Ms. Bryce?"

Janelle nodded her head. "Yeah. You see, Dominique and me went out together yesterday afternoon and evening. We hit up a bar around nine o'clock. Dominique had a few drinks. Then she started flirting with this dude. Problem was, ol' dude's girl was at the bar, too. She kept telling Dominique to

190

stop. Then she told Dominique that she was gonna put a cap in her ass." Janelle frowned. "I think that girl followed Dominique and did what she said she was gonna do."

The officer took Janelle's statement. Then he thanked her for her information. Right after Janelle left, he grimaced. "I think this case just got a whole lot more interesting."

Five Days Later:

Carmen couldn't believe what her attorney was telling her. "You mean the charges against me have been dropped?! All of them?!"

Lamont Covington laughed into his phone. "Yep. Every last one of them. Another witness came in and clued the police in on who had really committed the crime. The perp confessed. Apparently Dominique was flirting with some woman's husband and the wife didn't like it. She threatened Dominique, then followed through with her threats. You have a *'Janelle Bryce'* to thank for all of this. She's the person who gave the authorities the information."

Carmen thanked Lamont and disconnected their call. Then she ran over to Janelle's room and began banging on her door.

191

As soon as Janelle opened her door, Carmen threw her arms around her and gave her a bear hug. She pulled back smiling. "Thank you, girl! You just saved my life."

A sheepish little grin materialized on Janelle's face. "I guess you were just sprung of those charges."

"Yep." Carmen playfully punched Janelle in the arm. "Why didn't you tell me, honey?"

"I didn't know for sure whether or not my statement would pan out in your favor. It's not like I knew the people's names. I just knew what had happened and the name of the bar we'd been in. I didn't want to get your hopes up for nothing."

Carmen hugged Janelle again. "Well, thank you all the same. You're a real friend, Janelle."

Janelle was starting to feel a little guilty over that friend part. *If Carmen finds out it was me who sent those pictures, she's never gonna think I'm her friend...not ever again.*

"What's wrong, honey?"

Her feelings of guilt began to overtake her. After everything that had happened, she realized that Carmen would never love her in the way she wanted.

"What's the matter, J?"

Janelle sighed. "It was me, Carmen. I was the one who took those pictures of Kevin and Dominique. I'm in love with you girl. And I was trying to break the two of ya'll up."

That definitely shocked Carmen. She frowned and said, "Wow. I never would've thought that. I been thinking all week that Dominique was in it all by herself."

"No. It was my idea. I was just using Dominique as a pawn in my game. She had thought that once you left Kevin, she'd be able to swoop in and get him back. I had thought that I'd be able to seduce you. But I see now that that ain't gonna happen. All I can say is sorry. I hope one day you'll find it in your heart to forgive me."

The old Carmen would've wanted to fight. But the new and improved version simply frowned, shook her head and said, "Well, thanks for coming clean. See you around."

As she watched the girl she'd fallen for walk away, Janelle knew there was a chance they'd never be friends again. *I might be a sinner, but I'm trying to walk a little straighter. At least I did the right thing.*

Later on that Night:

Carmen leaned back in Kevin's arms on the porch swing at Halo House. She'd just finished telling him about everything Janelle had done. Kevin couldn't believe it either. But like Carmen, he was happy that

Janelle had confessed.

Kevin tightened his arm a little around Carmen's waist in contentment. "I think we're done with the storms now, sweetheart. I love you so much, Carmen. I can't wait to make you my wife."

She smiled. "And I love you, too, Kevin." Then she sighed. "After serving all those years in prison, I never dreamed I'd find anyone to love me, but I *did* pray for a soulmate one day — in my heart, I wanted one. I guess the Lord heard me and he sent me you on the wings of a prayer."

Kevin dropped a soft kiss on the top of Carmen's head. "Most definitely, babe. Most definitely."

PILOGUE

Two Years Later:

Carmen had tears in her eyes as she stood hand in hand with her husband of a year and half on an Atlanta sidewalk.

"You didn't sweetheart." she said.

Kevin wrapped his arms around Carmen's waist and kissed her soundly on the lips. Then he pulled back and smiled. "Yes, I did, Carmen Pittman...Attorney at Law. You fought hard and God blessed you to pass the bar...and with flying colors I might add." His smile widened. "I figured the least I could do was to get you your very own place to practice out of."

Carmen teared up again when she glanced back over at the words in the window of the building: *Carmen F. Pittman, Attorney-At-Law.*

He kissed her again. Then he took her hand into his. "You wanna go inside and take a look?"

She was excited. She bobbed her head up and down. "Of, course I do."

As soon as they stepped inside and flicked the

lights on, a loud cacophony of many voices shouted, "SURPRISE!!!!!"

Yep, she teared up again. Everybody that she loved was in there with party hats on and streamers, surrounding a big cake that read: *Congratulations Carmen, Attorney at Law!* Above that, a banner was hanging from the ceiling that read: *WE LOVE YOU!*

Lisa and Janelle rushed Carmen and gave her hugs.

Carmen had forgiven Janelle for what she'd done. Carmen's spirit had kept telling her to do so. Her spirit had kept telling her that Janelle would be a lifelong friend. She'd been praying real hard for her girl, and the prayers were working. Janelle had deserted her lesbian lifestyle six months ago and had become an active member of the church.

As for Lisa, she'd eventually sold the expensive Mercedes-Benz that Big Ron had bought her during the time they'd been a couple. She'd gotten about forty grand from the sale and had used the money to open herself up a bakery. It was called Divine Desserts. She'd been keeping God in the center of everything she was doing, so of course her business was thriving.

Mrs. Ridley had ended up telling Kevin and her husband the truth about Kevin's paternity. It had taken Kevin awhile to get used to the idea that Nathan was his father. Since Nathan hadn't known anything about the child he'd helped create, Kevin hadn't been angry at him at all. But he *had* been salty towards his

Aunt Michelle for several months for not telling the truth sooner. Kevin — being the man of God that he was — he'd eventually forgiven both his mother and his auntie for their deception.

As for Kevin's ex, Dominique, she never did regain the use of her legs. All Carmen could feel was sorry for her.

Smiling, Carmen dabbed at the tears in her eyes. A lot of the crying she was doing had to do with her pregnancy. She hadn't told her husband about their baby yet, but she figured she was about five weeks along. *He's gonna have a surprise himself when we make it home tonight. I'm gonna tell him about our son or daughter.*

"You okay, sweetheart?" he asked.

Carmen nodded her head. She had loving friends and family. She felt abundantly blessed.

FIRSTMAN PUBLICATIONS

Thank you for reading this book. On the following pages, we've provided previews of other great books by this author — stories that we feel you will thoroughly enjoy. Also, feel free to visit our website at **WWW.FIRSTMANBOOKS.COM** to:

*Register for FREE offers

*Sign up for our mailing list

*Check out additional great books by other Firstman Publications featured authors

*Order a FREE catalog

OTHER BOOKS BY WAYNE COLLEY

Trouble All In My Way

God Ain't Playing

A Diva's Prayer

Other Wayne Colley Books You May Enjoy

Firstman Publications   www.firstmanbooks.com

ON THE WINGS OF A PRAYER

Firstman Publications, P.O. Box 14302, Greensboro NC 27415
Email: firstmanpublications@gmail.com
www.firstmanbooks.com

DATE: _____

BILL TO

NAME _____ COMPANY _____
ADDRESS _____
CITY _____ ST _____ ZIP _____
Phone(___) _____ Fax(___) _____ E-Mail _____

SHIP TO

NAME _____ COMPANY _____
ADDRESS _____
CITY _____ ST _____ ZIP _____
Phone(___) _____ Fax(___) _____ E-Mail _____

Book Title	Item Code	How Many	Price Each	Total Price

☐ Money Order enclosed payable to Firstman Publications -OR-

Credit Card Number _____

Name on Card _____

Expiration Date _____ CVV Code _____

Signature _____

TOTAL AMOUNT	
SHIPPING: $3 for one book. $1 each additional book.	
SALES TAX: N.C. Add 7%	

GRAND TOTAL

43486820R00120

Made in the USA
Middletown, DE
25 April 2019